BATH & NORTH EAST S  **KU-387-566**

None Faster

Jim Allard arrived in Casa Grande bleeding and bruised and that was just a foretaste of what was to come. The problem was that he had killed a man known as the fastest gun alive and there was no shortage of men willing to test his prowess.

He was a man who knew cattle and enjoyed his job but what he wanted and what happened were two very different things. Rustlers, outlaws, crooked lawmen – all crossed his trail and there was plenty of hot lead to dodge before he learned the true meaning of the words *None Faster*.

CHAPTER 1

WELCOME TO CASA GRANDE

He was still bleeding from the fight when the train pulled into Casa Grande and he saw the lawman waiting in the shade of the high-stand water-tank.

The sun flashed from the star pinned to the worn but clean vest and the man took one last drag on his cigarette, flicked the butt into a small muddy pool beneath the dripping canvas hose, hitched at his gunbelt and sauntered up to the siding where the first passengers were alighting.

Jim Allard grunted with stiffness and bruising as he gathered up his saddle and rolled back the box car door – on the opposite side to the depot buildings. He dropped the saddle and jumped down, regretting it as his bones sent the jarring impact surging clear through his body. As he stooped to pick up the saddle, a shadow moved across it and a dusty boot

5

without spurs planted firmly on the embossed leather.

'Depot's t'other side, friend.'

A deep voice, confident, making it clear the owner didn't expect an argument. A solid, medium tall man, fortyish, a smudge of grey at the temples beneath the high-crowned hat. Allard thought immediately, *sensitive about his height.*

He straightened without attempting to jerk the saddle from beneath the lawman's boot, looked into a pair of hard blue eyes that had seen drifters by the score dropping, ticketless, out of empty box cars. Those eyes narrowed a shade as the man looked into Allard's face – looked up into Allard's face, for the drifter was a couple of inches over six feet and it was all rawhide muscle beneath his worn and dusty range clothes.

'Horse died under me in the badlands, Sheriff. Train was stopped at Papago Tanks when I stumbled in.' He gestured to the box car. 'Door was standing open – both doors – and all I could see was one big empty car and feel my two aching legs. And the knot in my empty belly.'

The lawman held his gaze steady, then looked down at the saddle, pointing with one rigid forefinger – on his left hand. His right stayed close in against the butt of the holstered six-gun.

'What's that oval thing on the pommel?'

'Silver plate.'

The lawman leaned down and examined it briefly, stiffened as he straightened fast, right hand closing around the Colt's butt now.

'It says "*Jubal Clay – None Faster*".'

'That's what it says all right.'

'Well. . . ?'

Allard shrugged. 'Won it off Clay in a poker game – in Price, Utah.'

'Jubal Clay – the "None Faster" says plenty about him.'

Allard shook his head. 'You're making the mistake most folk do – it don't refer to his gun speed. There was a horse race, clear across the Andeman Desert. Clay won. Left a string of eighteen others dragging ass behind him.'

'And killed a man right after – yeah, I know about that hoss race. Most of the country does. Seems the second placer reckoned Clay cheated. And Clay out-drew him, killed him on the spot. Seems to me that 'None Faster' could've been engraved on that plate *after* that difficulty.'

Allard shrugged. 'Wouldn't know about that, Sheriff. But Clay got into a card game I was in and it come down to me and him and he was cleaned out.'

'What happened to his race winnings?'

'You'd have to ask him. But he was sitting on three aces, a jack and a king, wasn't about to throw in his hand. He put up his horse and saddle – I had four queens.'

'Jee-*sus*! Wonder he never drew on you.'

'Not with a whole bar-room looking on. It was fair and square. He didn't seem that way inclined, anyways.'

The sheriff regarded Allard closely.'What happened to Clay? He just disappeared.'

'That he did. I rode out next morning, heading south-west – till my bronc gave out. Word was along the trail he got real drunk and picked a feller who wasn't faster on the draw than him, but he was stone cold sober. Clay went down to him and the feller lit out, no name, nothing. Said he didn't want to be known as the man who'd downed Jubal Clay: the whole blamed world would be after him to test his speed.'

The lawman Allard had seen first under the water-tank sauntered up, nodded to the sheriff who only came to the deputy's wide shoulder, and raked the drifter with a hard glare.

'Toss him in the cells, Jake?' He sounded eager.

The sheriff held up his hand without looking at him.'In a minute, mebbe, Duff. You got a name?'

Allard told him and the sheriff smiled crookedly.

'You know, you wear that gun like a man knows how to use it, Allard.'

'I've always worn it this way.'

'Which is neither denial nor confirmation of my remark. You know what I think? I think *you* could be Jubal Clay and just don't want it known.'

The deputy was straight as an arrow shaft now, surprise showing on his cocky face. '*This* is . . . Clay?'

'Could be,' the sheriff said, still drilling Allard with his gaze. 'We'll come back to that. How come you got fresh blood all over you, mister? Cut lip and cheek, bruise on the jaw. . . ?'

Allard hesitated – a mite thrown by the attitude of these lawmen. He sighed: he might as well tell them, but would they believe him? They were both mighty sceptical.

'Riding the box car, half asleep, when I heard footsteps up on the car roof. Went suddenly quiet and I knew whoever it was had swung over the side and was coming for the open door, hand over hand along the roof edge.'

'You thought of that right off, huh?' rasped Duff. 'Never for a minute figured he could've fell off; right now be lying hurt or dyin' beside the track?'

'Never for a minute.'

Allard recalled that moment when the scraping boot sounds stopped. The car was swaying along, the train moving fast, downgrade from the ridge of mountains behind Casa Grande. He heard the boot toes tap against the side of the box car twice, three times, and he knew whoever it was up there was handing-over-hand along the roof edge, planning on swinging himself through the open door – and surprising whoever was inside.

Allard himself had done it once, when he was hunting a man down near El Paso. So he started to his feet and was halfway there when the intruder came swinging through, just as he had pictured he would. A rawboned, dusty man in worn, dusty clothes, and a knife in his hand. As soon as he saw Allard moving he reversed his hold on the blade and threw the knife with intent to kill. Allard had good reactions, dropped flat, heard the blade bury itself two inches deep in the hardwood wall behind him. He lurched up, swinging the saddle with him, riding it up into the front of the still charging ranny. The pommel took the man in the midriff and doubled him over.

9

Allard dropped the saddle, lifted a knee into the dusty face and when the man straightened out of his jackknife, let him have a right and a left in the face.The man was no fighter: leastways, he had no stomach for trading punches with Jim Allard. He flung himself towards the wall where the knife had barely stopped quivering, yanked it out and came around crouching, blade angled upwards.

Allard skidded to a halt in mid-charge, but wasn't quite fast enough. The blade sliced through his shirt as his corduroy jacket flapped, and hot blood flowed. He twisted around and the attacker was still lunging and started to slide past him. Allard stuck out his leg and the man tripped, went down all a'tumble, arms and legs flailing. Jim didn't know where the knife was now, but he got in a couple of good kicks – until this tough, skinny *hombre* came up with a length of two-by-four lying in a small pile of offcuts in one corner. It clipped Allard across the shoulder, bounced up alongside his jaw. The rough-sawn end rammed at his eye and he felt it burst the skin and rip his eyebrow, splinters digging into the thin layer of flesh. Then it whistled past his head as he dropped into a crouch, bounced up right in front of the killer, *inside* his arm so that the length of timber was over Allard's shoulder, unable to club him.

He remembered grinning tightly in triumph before he butted the man in the face with the top of his head, jerked a knee up into the bony crotch. The man screamed and sagged. Allard grabbed the dusty coat lapels in both hands and with a roar of effort, heaved him out the open sliding door. It was rolling back and forth with the rocking motion of the train and the intruder hit his head on the iron edge before flailing out into the sunlight. Allard, sagging in the doorway, breathing louder – almost – than the panting locomotive, saw the body smash into the dry brush, dust rising before it was lost to sight as the train sped on.

He realized he had been silent for too long after explaining. The deputy, Duff O'Keefe, drew his Colt and hit him hard in the ribs. 'Sheriff asked you a question!'

Allard grunted, grabbing his side – and the sheriff saw the blood on the shirt, pulled the jacket flap aside.

'That what the knife done to you?' At Allard's nod, the sheriff told Duff, 'Ride back up the track and see if you can find this dusty man with the knife – which, I suppose, you no longer have?'

Jim Allard shook his head.

'Be handy for evidence.'

'I think it must've fallen out of the car; I never found it. Anyway, I'm not bringing charges even if you find the son of a bitch, so it hardly matters.'

'Duff, I told you what to do. Now move.' The sheriff watched the surly deputy give Allard a bleak look and then move off. 'I'm Jake Bartells, sheriff here. Fact is, I come specially to meet this train – just to see you.'

Allard stiffened, wadding a kerchief over the knife slash in his side. 'I don't know you, Bartells, and I'm not on any Wanted dodger, far as—'

He broke off and Bartells smiled faintly. 'Far as

11

you know, huh? Sounds interestin' – 'specially as I got a lot of questions to ask you about some rustlin'. And the murder of three good men, south of Tucson, not far from the San Xavier Reservation – reckon you can help me out?'

Allard hesitated just briefly, but saw that it sharpened Bartells' gaze and next instant he felt the Colt's muzzle pressing against his ribs, close to the knife wound.

'I don't know anything about rustling or murders.'

'Well, I reckon I'll find out for sure one way or t'other by sundown. Come along, Allard. And bring that fancy saddle. I'll find a place for it in my junk room.' He grinned tightly, adding, 'Might be kinda crowded in the cell bunk with you. Let's go.'

But Bartells wasn't that hard, only being tough. He let Allard sit in the chair opposite his desk, the saddle lying against the wall near the gun cabinet. He had relieved the drifter of his six-gun but merely laid it on the desk top near his hand as he dropped into his chair.

'Never seen this knife-throwin' man before, you reckon?'

'I said I didn't *know* him. I'd seen him at Piccolo Springs when I brought in a small herd of cows.'

The sheriff waited, face unreadable.

'He was in the livery when I stabled my bronc – not mine, strictly speaking, belonged to the man who owned the cows.'

'Lent it to you to make the drive: OK. This dusty man . . .'

12

'He watched me unsaddle—'

The sheriff gestured to the rig on the floor, arching his eyebrows, and Allard nodded.

'Yeah, that one. Seen him again in the saloon bar when I was being paid-off. The boss bought me a couple of drinks.'

'Hell almighty, Allard, gettin' the facts outa you is like pullin' teeth! Only the pain's in my butt instead of your mouth – but that could change.'

Allard smiled faintly. 'You don't need to come on so tough, Bartells. I can see you're a hard man.'

'You better believe it, mister. A lot have made the mistake because I ain't so tall . . .' He let it drift off. 'Reckon that feller spotted the silver plate and figured he could get some money for it? Specially with Clay's name on it.'

'Could be.'

'Well, you're a tryin' man, Allard, so s'pose we leave that and you tell me what you're doin' in Casa Grande?'

'It's where the train brought me. I didn't know where it was going when I jumped it at Papago Tanks.'

The lawman studied him silently while Allard rolled a thin cigarette from a near-empty tobacco sack. He offered it to the lawman but Bartells shook his head, took a cheroot from his pocket. He lit both smokes.

'Be interesting to know how you knew I was on that train, Sheriff.'

'Not you particularly, just a feller who was spotted climbin' aboard at the Tanks. You come outa the

13

desert – same place the fellers who rustled a herd and killed the trail men disappeared.'

'I'm a drifter. I do all kinds of ranch work and trail work. I don't throw a wide loop and I don't kill anyone who's not trying to kill me.'

It was said simply, at normal voice, without any fancy inflections. It was how an honest man would protest his innocence.

'You make it sound pretty good. But you could be smart enough to do that.'

'For Chris'sake, Bartells!'

The sheriff's right hand lifted a few inches off the desk top. 'Settle down, I'm just doin' my job. While you're in my town, you'll do what I say; answer my questions; jump through hoops. Or . . .'

The sheriff jerked his head slightly towards the door leading to the cell block. 'We'll just set a spell till Duff gets back.'

'I got nowhere special to go.' But Allard's eyes slid unconsciously towards the saddle with the pommel and the silver plate.

Bartells noticed. 'Stony?' When the drifter nodded, he asked, 'If you drove in cows to Piccolo Springs, what happened to your pay?'

'There was this flame-haired bar gal, skin like ivory, eyes green as emeralds . . .'

The lawman smiled crookedly. 'An' long fingers that could reach deep into a man's pockets, huh?'

'Told you the boss bought me a couple of drinks. Puma piss. Funny, I got a different impression of that gal now: hair was kinda straggly when I come to think of it; green eyes, but the whites were yellow; skin might've looked different if she'd had a bath . . .'

Bartells laughed shortly. 'Know that "after" feelin'. Serve you right . . . Guess you could use a cup of coffee.'

He called loudly and a young Indian girl appeared in a second doorway. Bartells gave her orders and she came back soon with a tray that carried a pot of coffee, two cups, and a plate of warm biscuits.

Allard's belly growled and his mouth was suddenly full of saliva.

He had eaten four biscuits and drunk two cups of coffee when Duff returned from his search. The dusty man was with him, face battered and smeared with dried blood, limping, his nose hammered over to one side of his face, left side of his head swollen around a shallow cut. His clothes were grimy, broken twigs and dead leaves still adhering to the worn cloth.

He looked exhausted and Duff toed out a straight-back chair and pushed the man down into it. The deputy looked at Allard.

'This the one?'

'Yeah. Bit more beat-up than when I threw him off the train.'

'Tried to kill me, the son of a bitch!' the dusty man snarled, all eyes on him now. He lifted a skinny arm, pointing a shaking hand. 'He's the one led us on that rustlin' raid! Double-crossed us all! After killin' the traders, he shot my two pards, but I managed to get away. Just luck I jumped the same train as him!' He slanted his wild eyes towards the sheriff. 'I know it'll cost me jail time, but I'll tell you all you need to know, just so long as it nails this murderin' bastard!'

CHAPTER 2

ELLA

Allard had rolled the last cigarette he could from the few flakes of tobacco remaining in his sack. It took only a minute to smoke. He was scrubbing the remains under his boot on the flagstone floor of the cell when Deputy Duff O'Keefe appeared at the barred door, unlocking it.

He jerked his head and took Allard back into the front office where Bartells sat behind his desk. There was no sign of the dusty man.

'Cuff him, Jake?'

'The hell for?'

'Well, rustler and murderer . . .'

'Go stand guard over Tole at the sawbones'. Relieve Hayes.'

The deputy went out, face tight, eyes flat as they swept briefly over Allard now sitting in the same chair as earlier.

'What's that ranny's name? The one I threw off the train?'

Bartells waved a dog-eared Wanted dodger. 'Bumper Tole – part Injun, Apache, I'd say. Known rustler and suspect in a couple of murders.'

'And you take his word above mine?'

Bartells sighed. 'He tells a good story.'

Allard waited, but not for long. The lawman said Tole claimed he'd been running with a small bunch of outlaws near Ajo, a two-men-and-dog town west of Tucson and not far from the big Papago Reservation at San Xavier.

'Small-time bunch. They been rousted from a half-a-dozen places, originally from up north someplace. Tole says you come driftin' into their camp, said a feller named McEwan sent you.'

'Bush McEwan?' Bartells frowned, snapping his head up, nodding gently. 'Heard of him. Never met the man.'

Bartells was slow to move his gaze from Allard's bruised face. 'Most folk've heard of Bush, I guess,' he conceded. 'Spent more'n half his life in prison but never seems to learn.'

'I wouldn't use a fool like that as any kind of a recommendation.'

'Guess not. Anyway, Tole said right off you started to take over, fought with their leader, Black Tom Gannon, an' killed him, so that made you boss and you led the gang on a few rustlin' raids, the last one on that small trail herd, where you killed the cowpokes and when Tole, an' his pards, bein' the upstandin' citizens they are, protested, you cut loose and shot two but he got away. Found out you were on the train from the Tanks and decided to square things.'

'That's his story – and you believe him?'

'Tole'd lie if he was caught with a wallet in his hand while the owner lay dead at his feet.'

Allard released a slow breath. 'I'm kind of glad you know his reputation.'

'Why you think he'd make up that story?'

'I beat him; threw off the train – vindictive. I dunno . . . How were his facts? About the raid and the killing?'

'Close to what we know – I'd say he was there. Could be they got away with the trail money: the herd had only been travellin' for a couple days and not much of the money would've been spent. Believe it was a coupla hundred. Big stuff for a rat like Bumper. Likely killed his pards, made a run, blew his stake in Piccolo Springs . . . and saw you with a saddle that had a silver pommel.'

Allard released another long breath. 'Nice to see we think alike, Sheriff.'

'It's a possibility, is all. I'm duty-bound to check out Tole's story. Oh, don't worry, he'll be goin' behind bars.' He flapped the dodger. 'Plenty here he's wanted for.'

'But you've still got to check.'

'Don't sound so peeved. Our cells ain't bad.'

The drifter stiffened. 'You gonna hold me?'

'Just while I check out Tole's lies.'

'Judas, you know they're lies already!'

'I dot my "Is" an' cross my "Ts", Allard . . . unless you can convince me you couldn't've been near that trail herd when the raid took place. . . ?'

Allard remained silent.

'Was two months back, along the Gila, near Painted Rock,' the sheriff prompted, and waited.

Allard scrubbed a hand idly around his stubbled jaw, thoughtful, but still silent.

'Mebbe you were up to somethin' else that don't bear lookin' into,' Bartells suggested, and saw Allard's blue-green eyes seek his face.

'Mebbe I was.'

'Well, if you were, I advise you to tell me now. I ain't foolin', and if it looks like Tole is even halfway right, I'm gonna nail your hide to the fence post.'

'Jesus, why d'you *hombres* work so damn hard at hearsay and skim over the truth?'

'I duuno as I've heard anythin' I recognize as truth yet.'

'I'll go along with that, if you're talking about Tole.'

'Forget Tole: worry about yourself.'

'I am worrying, the way you're looking at things.'

Bartells spread his arms. 'I'd say it's your move, Allard.'

There was a short silence and Allard lifted his head, about to speak, when the door opened and someone came in quickly. The drifter couldn't see who it was because the newcomer was silhouetted against the bright sunlight of the street before the door closed and brought cool greyness to the office once more.

'Jim Allard! Why didn't you go straight out to the ranch? I got to town too late to meet the train, but just heard in the general store that Sheriff Bartells had you in his office. . . . Would you like to tell me why, Jake?'

The young woman who had spoken so rapidly now turned towards the sheriff, and Allard, a little stunned, saw she was wearing a buckskin vest over a checkered blouse tucked into the waistband of a mid-length buckskin riding skirt. She would come up to his shoulder – in her high heels – he reckoned. The flat-brimmed hat hung down her back by a rawhide thong, partly obscured by the falling waves of jet-black hair. Her face, as much as he could see of it in the office dimness, was lightly tanned, maybe with a sprinkling of freckles across the nose, and her rather wide mouth spread now in a smile.

He thought it looked a friendly smile.

'Ella, you ain't s'posed to come bargin' into my office this way when I'm questionin' a suspect,' began Bartells, his clipped tones sounding sour, and he looked it.

'Suspect?' She turned the full force of her brown eyes upon Allard's rugged face, then flicked them back to the lawman. 'Suspected of what? You must have the wrong man, whatever it is, Jake. Jim Allard is on his way to work for me.'

Bartells frowned. 'You know him, Ella?'

'Well, of course I don't know him! But he's been recommended and sent by Purvis and Dalgetty. You know?'

'I know! The law firm in Flagstaff that handles the cattle business of most every ranch in south-west Arizona.' The sheriff rounded swiftly on Allard. 'Why didn't you tell me, damn you? If you come recommended by Purvis and Company, you have to be above-board, the way Old Man Purvis screens the

20

people he sends down here. Why you playin' with me, Allard?'

'Guess I'm just cantankerous, Sheriff. You had no need to keep me in a cell while you checked on Bumper Tole.' Bartells grunted, eyes narrowed. 'So you figured to teach me a lesson, huh? Give me the run-around!'

The woman gave a short laugh and Allard could tell it was forced – wondered if Bartells could, too? The sheriff was no dummy, so likely knew. And he glared at Ella. There was a lot of dislike there – if not raw hatred.

'Oh, don't be so techy, Jake! You know you can be a mite too officious at times – a lot of times! I've been waiting for Jim to arrive. Can he come with me now?' The lawman hesitated and she added a little impatiently, 'Surely there's no need to hold him any longer! Why, the thought of even doubting Jim against the word of scum like Bumper Tole!'

'OK, OK,' Bartells lifted a hand. 'I'm makin' you responsible for him, Ella! I still aim to check him out.'

'Good luck.' Allard stood abruptly, hitching at his gunbelt. 'How about my Colt, Bartells?'

The sheriff took the gun out of a desk drawer and skidded it across the desk. It slid off but Allard caught it long before it hit the floor. 'Damn good reflexes.'

'Practice.' The drifter holstered the gun and adjusted his hat, looking squarely at Ella for the first time. 'I'll just get my saddle, but I'll need a mount.'

'We'll hire one at the livery.'

'Thought you'd've brought one with you, Ella – if you was comin' in specially to meet this feller.'

'I drove the buckboard. I have a lot of gear to pick up at Godfrey's – it's going to be crowded.' She smiled. 'Jim has more the look of a rider than a passenger.'

Outside the law office, Allard toted the heavy saddle and said, 'Where's your buckboard?'

She pointed and they crossed the street to where the vehicle was being piled-up with kegs and boxes and sacks outside Godfrey's General Store. He heaved the saddle on top of some sacks of flour, settling it firmly.

'You can squeeze in after all. If you want.'

'I don't mind riding up front with you – give me a chance to find out who you are.'

Ella smiled. 'Ella Jones: spinster-name *Clay*.'

Allard stopped dead. 'Clay? Not—?'

'Yes, Jubal Clay was my brother.'

'But – he talked about a "kid" sister! You're—'

'All of twenty-four and a fallen woman – that is, I'm divorced, although I tell folk around here I'm a widow.' She laughed quietly and it wasn't forced this time. 'Jubal hasn't seen me in ten years; it's only natural he would refer to me as his kid sister.'

'Well, that's out of the way. Now, all you have to do is tell me how the hell you knew I'd be on that train when I didn't even know it myself.'

Bumper Tole had a bandage around his head and iodine had been painted over the cuts on his face. He was sitting up on a bed in Doc Willard's infirmary when Duff O'Keefe sauntered in, scowling at Hayes, the other deputy who was supposed to be guarding Tole. The man was standing, talking in a low voice to the doctor's nursing assistant, smiling, trying his luck.

'Hannibal,' growled Duff, his tone bringing Hayes around in a hurry. Duff jerked a thumb at the door. 'Jake wants you.' Duff softened his face and touched a hand to his hatbrim as he looked at the nurse. 'Sorry, Miz Halloran.'

Never knew when he might try his own luck there. She smiled, bobbed a part-curtsy and turned away, the long grey skirt swirling provocatively about the ample hips. The deputy looked away reluctantly as the medic came into the room.

'Come for him, Doc.'

'He has a slight concussion; I'd prefer to keep him here overnight for observation.'

Tole made his battered face hangdog and heaved a huge sigh which didn't fool the deputy at all. He walked to the side of the bed, grabbed the man's arm and dragged him to his feet.

'Duff! You stop that!'

'Doc, this one's a rustler and a killer – 'breed to boot. He overnights anywhere in this town it'll be in the cellblock.'

The doctor's seamed face hardened. 'Then you can damn well sign a waiver before you take him. It'll transfer all responsibility for his well-being to you.'

'You'll have to see Jake about that – I ain't signin' nothin'. C'mon, Tole.'

Duff grabbed the man's arm but he resisted, looking hangdog again in the doctor's direction. 'It's OK, Doc. I-I'll go along. Too sick to make any . . . troubled. But the bandage is too tight on my head. Restin' on the wound. Can you. . . ?'

'I'll adjust it.' The doctor moved to check the head bandage, passing briefly between the deputy and Tole.

Tole grabbed the medic, heaved him into O'Keefe who staggered back against a bench, knocking over specimen bottles and papers. The half-breed moved like a striking snake. He shoved the doctor hard, holding him against Duff, crowding the lawman. Tole had Duff's Colt in his hand as he dragged the doctor away and shot O'Keefe in the body. The deputy went down with a crash. Nurse Halloran screamed from the door. Tole leapt past the staggering medic, grabbed the woman and swiftly backed to the front door, dragging her down the passage, struggling.

'Quit that! Or I'll blow your spine in half!'

Nurse Halloran quit struggling but she was sobbing and shaking in fear.

He thrust her ahead of him into the street – just as Ella Jones's buckboard was passing on its way out of town, Allard sitting squeezed between her and two sacks of potatoes on the driving seat.

The sheriff was running down from his office, gun in hand.

Tole looked from the lawman to Allard who was trying to get enough room to palm up his six-gun.The nurse broke free and dropped to the boardwalk landing, falling off the edge to the top step.

Tole fired at Allard, the bullet absorbed by the sacks of potatoes. He lunged to the right as Allard pushed Ella out of her seat. She cried out in surprise as she fell, grabbing at the front wheel to keep from landing heavily. Allard stood and his Colt blasted. Splinters flew from the infirmary building as Tole ducked, triggered a shot under one arm. The sheriff fired but it was a shot into the air: he didn't want to hit any of the scattering citizens on the street. Allard leapt down from the buckboard, crouched as he ran to the rear. Tole dived for an alley mouth. Jim fired. The bullet knocked the 'breed against the wall. His lean body twisted, teeth bared with the pain of the body wound, smoking Colt lifting.

Allard's next shot knocked him sprawling into the street and the drifter ran forward, kicked the gun out of the man's hand. He had him covered by the time Jake Bartells came shambling up.

'Your damn reflexes seem to work well, Allard.'

'He's still alive, Sheriff – if you figure he's worth saving.'

The doctor came to the infirmary door, looking somewhat dishevelled, in time to help the nurse to her feet. She clung to him.

'Duff's been shot, Jake, it looks to be a bad wound.' The medic was moving back inside, leading the shaken nurse, as he spoke. 'Pull yourself together, woman! We have work to do!'

Bartells picked two men from the gawking crowd and told them to carry Tole inside. He watched Allard reloading his six-gun as Ella Jones came up, brushing dirt from her clothes.

'Sorry I was so rough.'

She had a smile for Allard. 'Not as rough as a bullet would've been. What happened, Sheriff?'

'I can't see through walls,' Bartells snapped, moving towards the infirmary. 'You folk go about your business now,' he told the crowd. 'I'll want to see you, Allard.'

'Not again!'

'Sheriff, we were just driving by when that 'breed started shooting! If it wasn't for Jim, who knows how many people he might have shot? Jim knows no more than I do.'

'I've got a report to fill out.' Stubborn.

They argued it back and forth for a short time and eventually Bartells agreed to let Allard continue on his journey to Ella Jones's Panhandle spread.

Once clear of town – at last! – she said quietly, 'You shoot well, Jim.'

'Well enough – not much speed, though.'

'Who can tell? You were jammed up against those potato sacks – and me. You hardly had room to move an arm.'

They drove on to a fork where a weathered sign-post pointed the way to Panhandle and several other ranches.

'Didn't realize there were so many ranches down this way.'

'You'd be surprised. Most folk figure this for useless cattle country but what we have here is a hardy breed – one that gives lots of meat that's quite tender. Maybe not as good as Texas or Montana beef, but it's coming into acceptance now by both the

meat houses and the public. I'm sort of experimenting with different breeds on Panhandle.'

'Success?'

'Not a lot. But I have hopes.' Her look was strange,
he thought. 'Jubal said you used to work for the King
Ranch in Texas.'

'Long time ago – or seems so. Now, there's a man
who likes to experiment with breeding.' He stopped.
'Now I get it. That's why Jubal wanted me to come
down here – delivering his silver saddle to you "as a
keepsake" was only part of it.'

She shrugged after a slight hesitation. 'It was his
idea. The note I got said little except you knew cattle
and had worked for King.'

'Now we're back to how you knew I was on that
train.'

'Really, I just took a chance. One of my men was in
the telegraph office when a message came through
for Jake Bartells, telling him a man who came out of
the desert, carrying a saddle with a silver pommel,
had jumped the train at Papago Tanks. They were
looking for some rustlers who disappeared in that
desert, but I thought it unlikely there would be two
drifters carrying such a saddle.'

Allard gave no sign whether he accepted this
explanation or not.

'Of course, I didn't know Bumper Tole would try
to steal the saddle.'

'I'm not sure what he was doing, except he wasn't
pulling his punches and would've killed me if he
could.'

Sober-faced, she said, 'I see the way you dealt with

27

him as a . . . good recommendation, Jim – for the job I have in mind. Although I knew Jubal wouldn't have sent you if you weren't able to handle yourself.'

A mile along the trail they came to a creek crossing and she halted the buckboard, allowed the team to rest and drink. 'Smoke if you want, Jim. There's time.'

He had no tobacco left so shook his head. There was something else he didn't want to tell her, too, but—

'One thing you better know, Ella.' When he had her attention he said slowly, 'I was the one killed Jubal Clay.'

CHAPTER 3

RELUCTANT GUN

It was just over three months ago now but seemed a lot longer. He had noticed lately, as he grew older, that time seemed to take strange twists and distortions, lengthening in the mind sometimes, at others, shortening drastically, so that something a year old seemed like yesterday.

Must be getting old . . . at 36?

It was a low point in his life. Things had gone wrong in a drawn-out sequence: mounts dying under him; caught up in fights he wanted no part of; losing at cards; being mistaken for a Texan outlaw named Macreedy and spending three weeks in jail before the law decided they'd made a mistake: Macreedy had been dead for weeks, gunned down in Deadwood, using another name. Allard never even got a 'Sorry'.

Empty pockets had put an edge to his usual casual ride through life. Nothing like your belly resting on your backbone to make you figure all these blamed laws everyone had to live by were just so much hassle to weigh a man down.

He had had enough: he needed money to live, so decided to live any way he had to as long as it made him enough to keep his belly filled and a horse under him.

It wasn't an easy decision: all his life he had been law-abiding. His Old Man had drummed it into him. 'Stick by the law, boy, and you'll always sleep easy.'

Made sense – until hunger gave a man a different slant. This time, it was a stubbled ranny who tried to jump him in an alley up in Utah. Allard knocked him senseless and, just as he was moving on, the thief had staggered out of the darkness, slurring, 'Wait! We can use a man like you . . .'

'We' was a small gang: mostly into rustling, the occasional stage hold-up, nothing very big, but once a Wells Fargo Express office. And that one nearly ended his career. The gang scattered. He found himself riding with a man who had never said much, kept mostly to himself, called Clay by the others.

On the dodge, at their camp deep in the Wasatch Mountains, he found out that Clay was the man's surname, not his first one as most men surmised.

'*Jubal* Clay! Hell, you've got a rep as a fast gun.'

Clay's face, caught in the flickering light of their small camp-fire, seemed to waver, his dark eyes glittering. The man stared at Allard for a long time. *Hell, was he going to go for his gun? He sure looked mean right at this moment . . .*

Then it passed and Clay's face slackened. He poked at the coals with a bent twig.

'You ain't what you might call a reg'lar outlaw, are you, Allard?'

Jim shrugged. 'Empty belly and pockets to match make a man a lot of things he mightn't want to be.'

'Way I figured you. I reck—'

Suddenly he gasped and fell off the log, writhing in agony on the ground, knees drawn up to his chin. Alarmed, Jim went to him, knelt, saw the man had bitten through his bottom lip, fighting some terrible pain.

'Wh-what is it, Clay? Can I help?'

Clay's eyes squeezed two wavering lines of tears, cutting clean trails through the grime on his face. Teeth bared, blood running over his chin, he shook his head once, breath gusting out of him. Allard reared back on his hams, thought it was the man's dying gasp as the eyelids sagged, the head lolled.

Slowly, Clay uncoiled his legs, jerkily, rubbing hard at his belly. His chest was heaving, the air whistling somewhere in the back of his throat. He lifted a hand and Allard helped him to a sitting position so he could lean back against the log.

'My left-hand saddle-bag – bottle. Flat. Brown stuff.'

Allard found it, read the label: *Laudanum.*

Clay looked at him as he removed the cork, swigged deeply. His breathing slowly settled and he held the still uncorked bottle on one thigh, watching Jim.

'You're the first one that's seen that – except for the goddamn sawbones in Salt Lake City.' He lifted the bottle slightly. 'He gimme this. No cure. Just

31

makes the pain bearable. He says! The hell does he know? He ain't got it.'

Allard pushed back his hat, rolled a cigarette.

'What is it? That's mighty powerful medicine – opium mixture. They give it to someone with cancer or such.'

Clay's eyes snapped. 'You know more'n I figured – it ain't exactly cancer.'

'What's that mean? Sounds like a gal saying she ain't exactly pregnant.'

Clay chuckled. 'Well, I know for sure that ain't my problem!' He coughed and grimaced, grabbing his belly. Took another swig.

'Easy! That stuff'll put you down with the devils.'

'I been there – an' it ain't all bad.' He paused for a long time. Allard lit the cigarette and put it between Clay's lips. The man nodded, squinting through the upcurling smoke. 'What the hell you doin' ridin' owlhoot, Jim? You just ain't the type – hungry, broke or otherwise.'

Allard shrugged. 'Just hit a low spot. Didn't give a damn. Truth is, sorry I joined up with that crew, but couldn't see a way out – till now.'

'Yeah. Grab this chance, Jim. I would, too, but it's way too late for me.'

Allard's eyes automatically went to the man's belly and Clay nodded. 'Old gunshot wound, b'lieve it or not. Never did get the slug out. It's caused some kind an infected ulcer that's eatin' me away – close to a goddamn cancer as you can get and still call it somethin' else.'

'You try any other sawbones beside the one who

gave you the laudanum?'

'A dozen.' The bottle sloshed as it was lifted, catching some firelight briefly. 'This is the best thing that come out of it. Used to ride up into the hills when I felt it stirrin'. Would go berserk. Shot more'n one hoss; left myself afoot, like a blamed fool. Any wildlife nearby din' have a chance. Outa my head with pain. Din' know what I was doin'. Now' – he twitched the bottle again – 'this does help some. Least the wildlife's safe.'

'What about a hospital? One of the big ones like Denver. Or—'

'Too late for operations. Just have to wait to die.'

'Chris'sakes! There must be something that can be done.'

'Nope.' He smoked silently until the tobacco burned his split lip, then spat the butt into the dying fire. 'I can't take much more of this, Jim. I ain't religious but I-I got a *thing* about a man takin' his own life.' He coughed and Allard realized it was meant to be a laugh. 'Me! A gunfighter, moralizin' about takin' life! Judas, I must've killed twenty men – more!'

Allard waited, smoking a cigarette of his own.

'You notice my saddle?'

'The silver plate let into the leather of the pommel? Saw it when I got your medicine. *None Faster.*'

'Not what you think. It's for that horse race across the Andeman desert—'

'Yeah. Was gonna enter but never got there in time.'

'I got a kid sister in Arizona. Ain't seen her in a while. Like her to have my saddle. I sure as hell got nothin' else to leave her. The silver plate might mean somethin' to her.'

After a moment, Allard said, quietly, 'You asking me to take it to her?'

'Yeah. She's on the family ranch. Likely give you a job. I'll write her a letter, tell her about you. I can't pay you.' His eyes glittered. ' 'Cept mebbe . . . in one way.'

Jim Allard frowned. 'What's that mean?'

'A way to get you a reputation that could pay off. Depends on you.' Clay was looking sharply at Allard.

Jim grasped his meaning. 'You're loco!'

'Could be. This damn pain makes me think some real loopy things at times. Look, we go down to a town, don't have to be a big one, 'long as there are some witnesses. We stage a small fracas an' it ends in us goin' for our guns, but you out-draw me and – you got yourself a reputation that'll bring in more dollars than you can shake a stick at.'

'You mean, be rich – like you?'

Allard sounded bitter, sardonic. Clay chuckled, coughed, tried to drink some medicine but it sprayed into the night.

'Damn wasteful of me! Jim, it ain't easy, bein' a top gunfighter, but it's where the money is and if you're smarter than I was you could end up rich.'

'Be able to afford a marble headstone instead of a pine board? I'm smart enough to know I want no part of such a crazy damn scheme.'

Clay sobered now, frowning deeply. 'I figured you

wouldn't jump at the chance, but I'd talk you around. I think mebbe I made a mistake.'

'I don't want to be a gunfighter – or an assassin.'

'No, see that now. OK, forget that stuff then. You'll take my saddle to Ella?'

Allard hesitated, then nodded.

'Good. Tell her she can unscrew the plate and mount it on a board if she doesn't like the saddle.'

They crossed over the Wasatch snow-capped ridges, Clay occasionally dropping back, once falling out of the saddle and almost rolling off a cliff in the throes of pain. He ran out of laudanum so they diverted to the small town of Price where he saw yet another sawbones. This man was a humanitarian who didn't like to see people suffer and gave Clay double-strength laudanum. 'At the end, it can make things easier,' the medico said quietly.

'Hell, you better watch that,' warned Allard.

'Hey, I feel good. You savvy what I'm sayin'? Good! Can't recall last time I could say that.'

Allard thought he seemed drunk, riding high up there, enjoying what time he had left. Well, he sure didn't have much to look forward to, so why not?

'C'mon, I'll buy some grub an' a drink – sody pop for me, I swear – an' we'll sit in on a poker game. Feelin' lucky, you b'lieve it?'

'How come you got money of a sudden?'

'Don't look like that. I been holdin' out on you, I guess. Feelin' you out and decided you're one to ride the river with. Quit lookin' so worried. I'll stake you.'

They were sitting on the creek bank now, the horses grazing in the shade of some willows, still hitched to the overloaded buckboard.

'It was some wad of cash, Jubal produced. Must've been two hundred at least.'

'Where did he get it?' Her voice sounded flat and her eyes were moist. She had hardly spoken since he had begun telling his story.

'I don't know, but he ran it into a good pile, then started losing and it was pretty damn obvious two other rannies in the game were setting him up.' He paused, then added. 'Jubal kept sipping that damn rotgut medicine and he got wilder and wilder, eyes red and burning. I tried to get him to fold and leave but he slapped my arm away and gritted his teeth at me: it looked pretty damn scary, 'cause his lip was still cut and swollen, bleeding slightly . . .

'I ain't foldin' – not till I get my money back from these two tinhorn card-sharps.'

A moment's dead silence – almost like a pause for respect at some important funeral – and then a chair scraped back and a card player hurriedly grabbed his few notes and coins and skedaddled, just as the two card-sharps rose as one, hands hovering threateningly over their gun butts.

'You got a bad mouth, mister!' the tall one snarled.

'Yeah, I have an' it's givin' me gyp. Must be because you two have been gyppin' me outa my dough.'

'By God, them's fightin' words!' snarled the smaller of the gamblers, starting his draw while the taller one stepped back and to one side, Allard thinking, They've done this before!

Not that it did them any good. Clay's gun whispered out of leather, thundered in a roar that shook the lampshade over the baize-covered table, even some cards stirring.

Allard was sliding out of his chair to one side, reaching for his gun, but it wasn't needed.

The two gamblers were hurled into contortions, even colliding and going down in a tangled heap as the lead smashed into them. Clay was grinning tightly through the gunsmoke.

'Gimme your gun!'

Allard hesitated:

'Come on! Gimme it, while you reload mine!'

The saloon was in chaos and Jim tossed Clay his Colt, the man picking it easily out of the air, throwing his own empty Colt underhand. Jim caught it, began shucking out the spent cases, thumbed in fresh loads just as the door crashed open and two deputies charged in, guns drawn.

It took them about a second and a half to pick out Clay under the swaying light at the card table, the dead men on the floor, Allard tossing the reloaded Colt to Jubal.

The deputies didn't hesitate. They started shooting on the run, bullets tearing up the table top, one smashing the lamp and spreading hot, burning oil on to the green baize. As it smouldered, Clay ducked, his own gun in hand now. Two shots and both deputies went down. Clay picked up a chair one-handed, hurled it at the barman who was trying to make up his mind whether to go for the shotgun under the counter. The chair bouncing off his head decided him and he dropped out of sight.

Clay was having a good time now, driving a shot into the crowd, a man falling and crying out, the rest scattering. Jim grabbed Clay by the shoulder and spun him round.

'For Chris'sakes! These men had nothing to do with it! Let's get outa here!'

But Clay's eyes were wild and red and crazy – maybe it was the laudanum, or maybe it was unbearable pain, maybe, even, simply a lust to kill.

Whatever, Clay rounded on Allard, shoved him back and brought up his smoking six-gun. He triggered and Jim Allard spun away, crashed against the wall, feeling the red hot searing in his upper chest. Then a bullet kicked splinters into his face and he instinctively thrust away from the wall, dropped to one knee, Colt coming across his body, left hand chopping at the hammer.

Jubal Clay was lining up his gun for another shot when Jim's lead smashed into his chest and drove him over a tangle of chairs. He slumped, back against the wall, shirt torn and bloody, gun lying in one hand, fingers curling loosely.

Allard straightened slowly, shocked at what he had done. The bar room erupted into talk and shouts.

'Nice work, feller!'

'Christ, who was that ranny?'

'He was ready to kill us all, the crazy coot!'

Allard dropped to one knee beside Jubal Clay and the man's eyes flickered open a little. Jim was never sure afterwards if he had been able to see him or not, but he caught Clay's last words as the man groped for his hand:

'*Gracias* . . *amigo* . . . give Ella—'

'That was all. Your name was the last word he spoke.' Allard stood and walked over to the creek, dropped to one knee and scooped up some water. He sloshed it over his hot face and then swirled a mouthful around his teeth, spat it out. When he turned, the girl was still sitting just as she had during his telling of the story.

Her eyes watched him now as he leaned a shoulder against a tree, pulled out his shirt and lifted one side, revealing a deep, twisted scar on the side of his left breast. It was still quite pink, not yet aged and puckered.

'This is where Jubal's bullet hit me. I just shot back without thinking.'

'That laudanam . . .'

He wasn't sure whether she was trying to find the reason for Clay's wild behaviour or looking for something to excuse it. But he nodded.

'Yeah, far too strong, but he needed it for the pain. Lucky he'd written to you and posted the letter off before he got into that card game.'

'And you brought me his saddle all this way . . . after he'd tried to kill you.'

'He didn't know what he was doing. And I'd already given my word.'

'Did the men in the saloon know who he was?'

'No. He just went by the name of Clay. Like me, when I met him, everyone thought it was his first name. We all just used one name mostly – Jim, Gary,

Keno, Spot. I never said who he really was though the sheriff suspected something. I tried to give the impression that Jubal was just a sore loser at cards – too drunk to know what he was doing.'

She dabbed at her eyes with a small handkerchief and he caught a whiff of some kind of perfume. 'You could've made yourself a reputation as the man who killed Jubal Clay – "None Faster". Strange that should've been the inscription on the silver plate, but referring to the desert race.'

'It was appropriate. I sure didn't want to be known as the man who killed Jubal Clay. The story would get twisted all round until it came out it was a square-off between Jubal and me. Then I'd've had every swaggering two-bit small town bully wanting to try my speed. Not for long, though.'

She frowned. Puzzled.

'Hell, I'm not fast with a six-gun. I can use one pretty good, shoot straight and so on, but I'm no streak of lightning. I'd've likely been dead after the first challenge. Gimme a rifle any day – I had to sell mine so I could eat a while back.'

'So it was you spread the story about someone who outdrew Jubal when he was drunk in an argument over cards.' She almost smiled. 'Pretty close to the truth at that.' Soberly, then, 'What happened to him?'

'I saw him buried in the Price Boot Hill, with a plain headboard. Used the balance of that money he produced outa nowhere. I put the name on the board as *Clay Gregg*.'

She drew in a sharp breath. 'Why did you use that name?'

'He told me it was his paternal grandfather's name, back in Kentucky, I think. But they'd named him Jubal after his mother's father. He said he would've preferred Gregg.'

She was silent and tears ran down her face. She wiped them away irritably.

'You— Jubal was right when he said he recognized you as a good man, Jim Allard.'

CHAPTER 4

TRUST

It was a long time since Allard had worked for a spread as big and as well run as Panhandle.

He had been here two days now and was riding the bay gelding supplied by Ella Jones. She had also given him a rifle and a workaday Denver saddle rig complete with provisions and bedroll.

'Here's a rough map of our boundaries and some landmarks. Ride around for a day or so and get the lay of the land, Jim. You'll see the special pastures I keep for the breeding stock. If you like what you see, you're hired.'

'You're mighty trusting. I mean, I've told you about the places I've worked – well, a coupla hundred of 'em, anyways.' He smiled crookedly. 'But I could be tweaking your nose.'

She laughed briefly. 'Give me credit for reading a man's character better than that! Besides, Jubal was never much of a letter writer, but his economy with words could tell as much as a page or two of a normal letter. He trusted you, Jim, and I see no reason why I shouldn't. You wouldn't've brought me the saddle if you weren't at least honest. And your knowledge of cattle more than satisfies me.'

He wasn't going to give anyone an argument about compliments like that.

And he was impressed with the Panhandle. There was a large crew – at least a dozen in the bunkhouse, but there had been five or six empty bunks, too, though faded pictures pasted to the wall above them told him their owners were just out on the range. The crew themselves seemed average, some overly friendly, some reserved, a couple indifferent, and at least one man hostile.

Mack Pendle, Ella's foreman. Maybe he was more suspicious than hostile, but Allard felt a wariness tighten his belly as the ramrod suddenly rode out of some timber on a bench that jutted out from a steep rise in the foothills.

A big man, Mack Pendle, with big, hard, scarred fists and a face that had been there and back a hundred times. He folded those big hands on his saddlehorn now, letting Allard approach. 'Go easy with the spurs on that bay.'

For reply, Allard kicked his right boot free of the stirrup and held it out: no spurs.

'Don't get smart with me, drifter.'

'Wouldn't be hard, but – OK. You're the ramrod.'

'Damn right. Think you're gonna fall into an easy job, don't you?'

'Haven't decided if I'll work here yet.'

'You will.'

The man was right, but Allard merely shrugged.

'And you'll take orders just like all the rest.'

'I've punched a lot of cows in my time, Pendle – even a few foremen, come to think of it.'

'Don't try that here!' Pendle glared, and there was no change in Allard. The foreman suddenly lifted an arm. 'Ride on over and you'll find the valley she keeps for what she calls her special herds. Babies 'em like a bunch of kids!'

'Ella sees the future of Panhandle in improving the breeds she's trying to develop.'

'Oh, is that so? You got her confidence, huh? Well, to me, that special herd is a bunch of deformed freaks and I reckon she's wastin' her money. And you're gonna help her spend it, anyway, ain't you?'

Allard smiled. Pendle was coming on hard, but now he could see beneath that raw surface: Mack was afraid of the new ranch hand. Not physically – it would take a lot more than someone like Allard to scare this ranny, if it could be done at all – but Mack was afraid Jim might worm his way into Ella's favour and oust Pendle himself. Maybe he had a thing for her. He was one of those tough men who didn't care whether he was liked or not, but could be damned loyal to his employer – if it would further his own interests.

'Worked for Panhandle long?'

The casual question caught Pendle off guard, then his face sobered. 'A lot longer than you'll be around. I come here near-starvin'. Old Man Clay gimme a job, practic'ly raised me. Aw, not like one of the family: he was a hard-nosed old bastard, but he taught me all I know.' Mack suddenly spat, giving Allard a straight shaft from those pale eyes. 'And I know a shifty drifter who figures he's just moved in on easy street when I see one.'

'Get your eyes tested, Mack. I need work, and I'll give value for dollar. And I won't be spur-raked, rode or bullied, beat-up or put-upon as long as I feel I'm doing just that.'

So there it was: lying between them like an opened package. It could be picked-up or trodden into the ground. It was Pendle's move.

And he made it: leastways, he moved. He grunted, wrenched his mount's head up, spurred alongside Allard, teeth bared, one hand on gun-butt. 'Don't you sass me, saddlebum!'

'You gonna use that gun?'

Mack wasn't sure if it was a challenge or not, but he was the kind of man who would have to read it that way. He whipped the gun free and swiped at Jim's head. Allard stretched out along the bay's neck, slipped a stirrup, right leg riding up while he took his weight on his left foot, at the same time drawing his Colt. Mack's blow knocked his hat off but Jim came surging back up and slammed the side of his gun across the ramrod's head. Pendle tumbled loosely out of the saddle. Sprawled on his back, he blinked up at Allard who had instinctively cocked his pistol.

Mack looked briefly afraid, shook his head swiftly.

Jim stared down at him, holstered his gun, then leaned down and picked up his hat without quitting leather. He kept looking at the downed foreman while he dusted off. Mack didn't move.

'I don't work on Panhandle yet, Mack.'

Allard set his hat on his head, nodded briefly and rode off towards the rise.

Something had been settled, though he wasn't sure what.

Riding back in the early dusk, Jim Allard saw a chestnut, still saddled, but with the cinch loosened, hitched to the corral gate. It was a horse he had seen before, outside the law office in Casa Grande. The stirrups were set for a medium tall rider.

Off-saddling the bay, he heard the front door of the big ranch house open. Ella Jones came to the top of the porch steps. 'Jake Bartells is here to see you, Jim. He's staying for supper. Eat with us.'

Allard nodded, washed-up at the bench alongside the bunkhouse where the weary cowpokes were gathering for their grub.

'With any luck the sheriff'll take you away and we'll be rid of you.' It was Mack Pendle, leaning against an awning post, still sneering. His face looked lopsided.

'Keep watching. You could be lucky.'

Pendle scowled as Allard strolled up to the house, running fingers through his thick wet hair. He went in without knocking.

Bartells nodded to Allard as the girl motioned him to a chair at the supper table. A young Mexican girl brought a platter of food. 'See what you think of my beefsteak, Jim.'

He smiled at Ella. 'Notice you got a predominance

of Whitefaces in your breeding herd up the valley.'

'Yes. Back in the '20s, my grandfather, Gregori – originally from the Balkans or some such place, changed his unpronounceable surname to Clay when he settled in Kentucky – imported the first Brahmans in the country from India, knew they had a reputation of being tick-free because he'd served there in the Britsh Army. He crossed Herefords with Longhorns, too – hence the Whitefaces.'

Jim cut the sizzling beef and was surprised at how tender and tasty it was. 'Taste is what's gonna sell your beef, Ella. Eat longhorn anywhere in the country and it's just something to chew – unless you smother it in sauce or gravy, you got no flavour. Ought to be a ready market for this.'

His remarks pleased her. 'Yes, there is, and if I can breed tick-resistance into my herd with Brahmans—'

'You could have a winning combination.'

But before the discussion could go any further, Jake Bartells said, abruptly, 'Bumper Tole died.'

Allard swivelled his gaze across the table, nodded soberly. The sheriff added, 'He did some talkin' first.'

Allard chewed and waited, the girl sitting very still now, trying to bring back her line of thought from her herd of specially bred cattle.

'Did you know he was in the saloon in Price when Jubal Clay went plumb loco?' The lawman turned quickly to the girl. He cleared his throat. 'Seems Tole knew Clay, had ridden with him in a wild bunch under Old Man Tole – "Cimarron" they called him. Bumper claimed Clay owed him money that he stole

47

from Cimarron, said he'd been short-changed after some robbery and when Bumper found out he won that Andeman Desert race, he reckoned to collect. When Clay gambled the winnings away, Tole figured he'd settle for the saddle and its silver pommel. Then there was the fracas in the Price saloon when Clay went off his head and Allard was the one finished up with the saddle.'

'So he jumped me on the train for it?'

Bartells narrowed his eyes slightly. 'Tole was full of likker more often than not. If he got downwind from a distillery he'd walk barefoot through a brushfire to get to its front door. He was loco drunk an' he was mad at you.'

'Is that why, when Duff found him, he accused Jim of rustling and murder, too?' Ella asked.

The sheriff shrugged. 'Reckon. Like I said, Tole's brain was pickled in rotgut. Allard'd thrown him off the train and I guess he just saw a way to get even with Jim. Wouldn't be the first man it's happened to.'

'Well it don't matter now.' Allard suddenly looked straight at Bartells who was hunched forward a little. 'Or does it?'

'You never did tell me what you were doin' when that trail herd was hit – the one Bumper claimed you raided. Ella came in just as I asked you. Oh, and I telegraphed Purvis Dalgetty in Flagstaff: they don't recall recommendin' this ranny to you, or anyone else, Ella.'

She flushed, toyed with her cutlery. 'I . . . may have stretched the truth a little, Jake, but I'd just received Jubal's letter and he was obviously impressed. I wanted Jim working for me. I'm sorry.'

'Well, if I didn't more'n half-believe Allard this wouldn't be such a pleasant evenin',' Bartells said, and it was the first warm smile Allard had seen the lawman give. Aimed at Ella. Then Bartells turned to Allard. 'I worked out some times and it seems you could've been with Jubal Clay around the time of that raid. Besides, Purvis said though he'd never met you he knew you by reputation. Seems the 'Jim Allard' name'll open a lot of doors in cattle country.'

'Well, thank you, Mr Purvis – whoever you are.' Jim sat back, watching the sheriff squarely. 'This your way of telling me I'm off the hook now?'

'For now,' Bartells corrected. But his crooked smile didn't hold much threat. 'Believe I told you I'm a man likes to dot his "Is" and cross his "Ts". But, for now, I'm satisfied you're tolerably law-abidin'. He's all yours, Ella – if you want him.' *There was something in the way he said that.*

'I need someone who knows and has worked with different breeds of cattle, Jake.' She flicked her gaze to Allard. 'Jim, I want you to look over a mixed-breed herd on a ranch at a place called Corazon, between Bisbee and Nogales. It's a long lonely ride, I know, but I'll give you fair pay.'

'I don't mind long rides. You got a timetable?'

'Three weeks, no longer than a month. It depends.' She glanced around, instinctively lowering her voice as folk do when they have something to say that they consider confidential. 'I've been experimenting with Herefords and Longhorns, as you know, but the man who runs the ranch I told you

49

about, Beau Norton, has Brahmans as well as a
Hereford seed bull in the herd. I believe he has
Durham Shorthorns, too, even one of Shanghai
Pierce's so-called Mossyhorns. But all I really want,
Jim, is that Hereford seed bull and the Brahmans.'

'You'll tip your hand if you just want me to bid on
them.'

'No, no, I realizie I'll have to make an offer on the
whole herd.' Her voice took on an edge of excite-
ment. 'I've been doing a lot of reading, sent to
Washington and London for some books, and I'm
convinced that if I breed correctly from the
Hereford, with my original longhorns, I'll be able to
pack up to an extra three hundred pounds of meat
on to the progeny. I'll need the Brahmans for tick-
resistance: with the four I already have in my herd,
Jim, I can speed up the process.'

They were silent at her words, Bartells looking
from Ella to Allard: the sheriff was out of his depth,
didn't know enough about cattle breeding to make
any worthwhile comment.

'King tried something similar but someone killed
his seed bull . . . I never heard he bought another.'

'What I'm afraid of is if King gets to hear
Beaumont Norton has *his* seed bull up for sale he'll
beat my offer.'

Allard pursed his lips. 'You're trusting me with a
helluva lot, Ella. I dunno that I'm expert enough to
make the sort of decision you want.'

'You'll know whether it's worth the gamble when
you see the bull, and the progeny, won't you?' There
was a slight tension in her voice and, while he didn't

really want this responsibility, he knew her disappointment, if he rejected her offer, would be devastating.

He had already heard bunkhouse gossip that she was dead-ended with her own experimental programme and funds were spread mighty thin – she had even asked the crew if they would accept only part-wages this month, until she could negotiate a loan from the Casa Grande Bank.

'I could give it a try, Ella, but I wouldn't feel right making a recommendation unless I'm about eighty per cent sure. And that might take time.'

She smiled widely. 'I can make my timetable a little more flexible, if need be,' she said, then lifted a small silver bell and tinkled it. The Mexican maid came hurrying in. 'Conchita, bring brandy with our coffee, please – the good brandy my father imported from France some years ago.'

'*Sí, señora* – I find some.'

As the maid hurried out Ella beamed at her guests.

'This calls for a toast in the finest liquor, gentlemen. Jim, you may not realize it, but you have just saved Panhandle and given it a future. Not to mention one for yourself!'

Allard said nothing: he wasn't confident that he knew enough to tackle this chore. It would mean a long, hot and hungry ride under a desert sun that would burn the eyes out of a cave-dwelling lizard, thirst that would shrivel a man so his clothes hung loose – and what would be waiting at the end?

The *possibility* that this Norton might have a seed bull as good as he claimed and, if so, could already have made a deal with King, the richest and most powerful owner of the biggest ranch in the US.

And Jim Allard had never had much luck at gambling.

But, while he might never admit it, he was too soft hearted to refuse Ella Jones, whatever the odds.

But what made him really uncomfortable was the way Bartells was looking at him, his face carefully blank.

Jim knew damn well the sheriff had read his mind. But there seemed to be something more there, too: in the curt way he spoke to Ella, and how when he looked at her while he thought she wasn't aware, well, it was kind of strange.

CHAPTER 5

SMELL OF GUNSMOKE

There was a smell of gunsmoke in the air. Not strong, but even though Jim Allard's nostrils had been abraded by the desert crossing and the scorching sun, he could still get a whiff.

He hadn't noticed it on the approach to Norton's ranch, riding over a small hogback and seeing the place spread out before him. It was medium size and the barn and outbuildings and corrals were in reasonable condition. But it had an almost neglected look, as if it was waiting to be brought up to the standard it should be and someone was too blamed lazy – or busy – to get around to it.

Maybe he was just irritable from that long, gruelling ride: he could sure do with a decent cup of coffee or a nice long drink of cool water from a deep well. His water supply had all but boiled in the canteen and if there was anything Jim hated it was drinking warm water. He must have downed gallons over the years.

It was as he rode into the yard that he caught the first faint whiff of gunsmoke: the gun or guns had likely been fired some time ago, hours, even last night. That's if his sense of smell was operating at its usual high capacity. And it had been a still night with no morning breeze to disperse the clinging powder-smoke smell.

There were two men standing in the shade of the barn, one flicking pebbles with thumb and forefinger, the other idly watching. They looked a lot like the spread itself – in need of a good scrub-up. They watched him blankly, no greeting, nor invitation to dismount. But he did so anyway, stiffly, loosened his cinch and eased the straps on the pack horse.

The one flicking the pebbles kept on performing his pointless exercise: he apparently had a good supply of pebbles in his jacket pocket. The other merely looked on, blew out smoke from a cigarette that hung from a corner of a thin-lipped mouth.

'Name's Allard – representing Mrs Ella Jones. I'm here to look over the herd Mr Norton has for sale.'

The men exchanged a look and the one flicking the stones stopped the amusement abruptly. 'Best go tell 'em up to the house, Cal. Wouldn't want to keep a "representative" waitin'.'

The second man, average-sized and unshaven, twitched his shoulders to straighten up and took his time sauntering up to the house. He opened the front door, leaned in and called, 'Wendell, we got us a visitor. Here to look over the herd.'

Allard waited, mopping his damp hair under his dusty hat with a balled kerchief, wiped the inner leather band. The other man started flicking his stones again.

'Hit a lizard yet?'

Cold eyes slowly moved to Allard. 'If I had one to shoot at, I'd hit him.'

'Thought you might use a six-gun.'

The man frowned. 'On a goddamn lizard? Ammo's cheap but not that cheap. . . . Why you say that?'

'Sort of smelled gunsmoke as I rode in.'

There was tightening of the slab face and maybe a compression of the thin lips as the hard eyes held to Allard's dirty face. 'Well – maybe. We was shootin' at a coupla rats early on.'

'Ammo not too expensive to use on rats, huh?'

Jim didn't flinch under the steady, now hostile gaze. 'I shoot whatever I like – whenever – wherever.'

'The sheriffs must just rub their hands waiting for you to hit town. They reserve a cell for you?'

'Listen, feller, I dunno what the hell's wrong with you, but you better watch what you're about while you're here.'

Allard heard boots on the porch and then crunching on gravel. There was a tall, lean man, hatless, sandy hair short and not too thick, coming towards him. The thin-lipped man had apparently gone into the house.

'You're who?'

'Jim Allard. Riding for Mrs Ella Jones of the

Panhandle spread, Pine County. You Mr Norton?'

'Yeah, I'm Beau Norton. She wants you to look at the herd?'

'If it's still for sale – and I sure as hell hope it is, after crossing that desert.'

Norton suddenly smiled. He had a long face, with a large nose, but there was something attractive about it: not exactly a welcoming countenance, but one that could quickly fit in to most situations and seem right at home, making everyone feel at ease. 'She's a bitch, ain't she?'

Jim felt a strange flutter in his midriff: he had a crazy thought that Norton might be referring to Ella and not the desert.

'How much time you got?'

Remembering the deadline Ella had set herself, only a month away, Allard told Norton he wanted to get the inspection over as quickly as possible.

'OK. Birch, you saddle a bronc and take him out to where we got the herd.'

'Want me to stay with him?'

Norton's smile widened, as he watched Allard. 'Nah. He looks like a man can do his chores and move on.'

Seemed to Jim like that was a bald enough hint. Strange way to sell a herd, and not even coming out with the prospective buyer. . . .

'You got papers? Your seed bulls, cows they've mated with, when, number of calves dropped?'

Norton frowned and Birch seemed to have a sudden thought. 'Lots of papers in that roll-top desk,' he said quietly, looking directly at Norton.

'Think they're among 'em.'

Jim frowned. Hell, the man ought to know where his breeding records were kept. This was a queer place. Not even offering him a cup of coffee: just wanted him out of here.

Norton seemed to remember something as Jim turned to his weary mount and tightened the cinch again.

'You authorized to buy the herd?'

'I can arrange a deposit through the bank in Bisbee. Mrs Jones'd have to make the final decision.'

Norton probed at a molar with his tongue as he said gently 'Well, thing is, I'm goin' to Mexico and want to get this settled soon as I can. If you figure the herd's good enough to leave a deposit on, you could get this Jones' woman's OK to have the bank pay me in full, couldn't you? Then you could drive 'em out or pick 'em up later while I get on down to Mexico and tend to the business that's waitin'.'

It was a bit odd, but not unreasonable. 'Let's see what your herd looks like first.'

'Sure. Birch, mebbe you better stay with Mr – what's your name? Allard? Stay with him and make sure he sees all the steers, OK?'

Steers? In a breeding herd? What the hell was wrong with the man?

Allard was more impressed than he expected to be, after seeing the general condition of the ranch – and the off-handed manner of Norton. He had not held much hope of finding the breeding herd in as good a shape as Ella apparently thought. 'If it's OK, I'll

57

camp out overnight.'

Birch stiffened. 'Here?' meaning the fenced-in canyon where the herd grazed. 'Hell, man, I got a nice warm bunk waitin' for me back at the spread.'

'Go ahead and use it. No need for you to stay.'

Suspicious, Birch asked, 'Why you wanta stay over?'

'Cows are like people – interesting to see them first thing in the morning just when they're waking up.'

Birch dropped a hand to his gun butt. 'You joshin' me?'

Allard shook his head. 'If the cows're a good breed and they've been looked after well – and these sure seem to have been – they oughta be bawling-in the day and moving around, looking for a drink and grass in their favourite spots. Frisky, in other words.'

'An' if they ain't?'

'It's not too important, but the slow-starters might not be as fit as they should be. Mating different breeds don't always work out. You have a fine-looking animal but the muscle structure ain't what it should be, or even the brain's too slow passing on its messages.'

Birch shook his head. 'Judas, you damn breeders are a queer breed yourselves!'

Now that was a strange thing to say for a man who was supposed to have been working with cross-breeding cattle.

By mid-morning, Jim knew this was the herd for Ella. Of course, a veterinary would have to do sperm checks and so on to be absolutely certain, but he had seen enough cross-bred cattle to know that Norton

58

had been successful here: which came as some surprise, for Norton hadn't impressed him as having either the patience or skill. And that Hereford was a massive beast, his ball-bag almost dragging on the ground, the eyes watching his every movement as he examined the cows and calves. The *bull's* cows and calves.

He had the impression that Norton was in too much of a hurry to stand still for a veterinary to run his tests, so Jim decided to take a chance.

Norton shook his head – as expected – when Jim mentioned bringing in a veterinary for semen tests and blood-cell counts. 'Man, I've been all through that. I found the papers you wanted. It's all there, written out – you want that bunch of critters, it'll cost your Mrs Jones ten thousand bucks.'

Jim Allard felt every fibre tighten. That might sound like a lot of money, but in the cattle-breeding business it was chicken-feed, up against the amount of work that must have gone into Norton's herd. Of course, Ella might still have trouble raising that amount, but the price should have been higher.

There was something queer about this Norton, and his crew. There were only four of them, the three he had met – if that was the word – and another ranny who had ridden in this morning, a half-breed, wearing an eagle feather in the back of his braided black hair. They called him Centavo. He looked meaner and more ravenous than any timber wolf Allard had made the acquaintance of. He was a walking cadaver and Jim had him tagged as a killer. He carried a big-bore rifle with him everywhere, contempt in his black stare. But he said little though his eyes shuttled quickly to Norton when the rancher named his price.

'I'll have to send a couple of telegraphs, get Mrs Jones's OK for the price and a deposit.'

'No. It's ten thousand cash – hers or the bank's, I don't give a damn – or the herd goes back on the market.'

'I still need to get those wires away.'

'Birch'll take you into town. See if she can give the local bank the OK to pay me.'

'I'll need your ranch account number if it's to be paid in—'

'Goddamnit, Allard! I said I want *cash*! Get her authority to have the bank pay me cash.'

'Mexico must look pretty good to you – ten thousand US dollars is gonna buy you a lot of tequila and *señoritas* down in *mañana* land.'

'What it buys us ain't no concern of yours. OK, Birch, get ready to ride into Bisbee.'

'Thought you might come yourself – you know, papers to sign and so on.'

'Birch can do that: I'll give him my authority.'

As he mounted the big bay, which he had rubbed down last night and generally groomed, Allard wondered why Norton was so leery about going into a town and a bank he must have done business with a hundred times over the years.

He couldn't put all his uneasiness – his *suspicions* – in the wires he sent Ella, just the facts.

She must have been excited for a reply came

within half an hour.

> Buy! Have OK for bank loan. Wiring authority for payment of cash as requested. Thank Norton. Bring records soonest. Sending trail crew. Ella.

It surprised Jim that she wanted him to come back and not wait for the trail crew, but it suited him. He didn't care much for Norton's company, nor the others.

That first sundown, he camped in a hollow among the dunes he had used on the way down. Norton hadn't offered him any vittles so he had bought some fresh grub in town before leaving. He was tempted to spend the night in a hotel room, but figured sleeping in a feather bed for such a brief time would only make it harder to face the lumpy bedroll out in the desert.

He spotted a jack-rabbit, shot it on impulse, and broiled it over his fire, but it was tough and stringy and jammed up his teeth. He spat out a last mouthful and leaned across to pick a sliver from a stick of kindling to use as a tooth pick.

That unpalatable jack-rabbit saved his life.

As he leaned across to the stick, something burned air close to his head and then he heard the boom of a rifle out in the night. Long experience on a thousand lonely trails had him kicking forward, continuing the leaning movement, boot toes digging in, legs snapping straight, launching him out of the firelight.

He rolled across his bedroll and snatched up his rifle that was lying on the blanket. Sand and gravel spurted in several eruptions as the bushwhacker's rifle boomed again and again out there. *Big bore! Centavo?*

'Why' could wait. Jarring to a stop behind a low ridge of earth, he levered a shell into his Winchester's breech, knocked his hat off and lifted his head warily. He thought he was blinded by the stinging gravel, hurled himself back and hugged the ground. It had been a fool move but he had seen the long muzzle flash of the gun out there. And that killer was mighty fast.

He had noted the place on the way in, had even thought of making his camp there: a small pile of rocks that would have protected him from the wind. But they were still sun-hot and would radiate too much heat because of their size. Besides, he had heard the buzz of a rattler warning him off.

The killer had chosen the spot because it was slightly higher than Jim's campsite and there was not much cover for him. In fact, he was situated in the only possible cover he could use. The ambusher had seen this, probably, and now raked the mound with a volley of four shots.

They were big-calibre bullets and he kept seeing that heavy rifle Centavo was carrying at Norton's spread. Light was bad but there was a faint afterglow and those rocks where the killer lurked were a darker blotch against the sky. He didn't see the man moving, but something ran across the top of a boulder: pack-rat, maybe, or – an eagle feather standing straight up from braided black hair on a crouching man.

Jim held his fire: why let the son of a bitch know he had spotted his position? Better to let him think he was still safely hidden and, when he lifted up for his shot. . . .

And there he was! Not only did Jim Allard see the line of the boulder broken by the killer's head and shoulders as he prepared to shoot, but he heard the clash of the lever action as the man slammed a shell into the breech.

Jim threw the Winchester to his shoulder and triggered four rapid shots, rock dust boiling over there, a clattering sound through the dying gunfire that might have been the big rifle falling – or Centavo's body.

He was wrong on both counts, it seemed, for the big rifle slammed three shots into his mound, chewing out fist-sized hunks, sending him sprawling. *By God that 'breed – if it was him – was lightning fast!*

Not only that, the man was moving – closer!

Jim didn't believe it. No one was crazy enough to jump to their feet and run forward into the face of gunfire like that. But that damn 'breed was doing it! He could see him clearly enough now, coming on like a charging buffalo, rifle butt braced into his hip, working lever and trigger.

There was no accuracy this way but all he intended was to make Jim keep his head down. Which he did, successfully. And suddenly the dirt and gravel where Jim lay was pushed against his body and over to one side and he knew the crazy breed was standing on top of the mound.

He twisted and looked up, into the big smoking bore of the murderous rifle. *Buffalo gun*, his mind registered and he knew one of those huge slugs at this range would take his head off. He was a breath away from Hell.

Then the big side hammer clicked on an empty breech.

Allard's Winchester swung up and the muzzle was no more than three inches from the 'breed's greasy buckskin trousers when Jim fired. The man was blown back completely off the mound, feet leaving the ground, body shuddering as the bullet tore upwards through his organs. Then he seemed to crumple like a sagging wet paperbag and sprawled across the mound.

Allard rolled away, automatically levered another cartridge and stood up – shaking.

There was no use questioning the 'breed – he would be dead within minutes, maybe seconds – but going through the man's pockets and rummaging amongst all the medicine totems he carried, Allard found two brand new fifty-dollar gold pieces.

Now he knew what his life was worth – but damned if a hundred lousy bucks seemed like a fair price.

CHAPTER 6

SUSPECT

A sandstorm coming out of the south-west delayed Allard's return. He cursed uselessly as the sand stung him and clogged his nostrils, mouth and eyes, drove his horse at an angle. Finally, he had to stop, the bay's rump turned into the scouring grey clouds.

He wouldn't have taken this trail except he had decided to stop in Casa Grande and tell Bartells about Centavo. It would come out sooner or later and even if the fussy sheriff wanted to hold him over, he could arrange for the breeding papers to be sent out to Panhandle. Or Ella could come into town and collect them.

He was delayed for over a day, driven far south in order to dodge the storm, and now had no choice but to pass through Casa Grande on his way to Panhandle. There seemed little use in not seeing the sheriff first.

Bartells listened silently, hard eyes watching Jim

every moment, occasionally cocking an ear at certain words.

'If you were suspicious, why did you go through with the deal?'

'No choice. Ella wanted those bulls before King got to hear about them and Norton – if that's who it was – wanted a fast sale so he could get to Mexico.'

Bartells leaned forward swiftly. 'You think this Norton was an impostor?'

Allard hesitated, then nodded. 'Pretty sure. Feller who went up to the house to call him, yelled "Wendell", but he introduced himself as Beau Norton.'

'That's who runs the spread, all right. Feller about my size, little younger, and with a longhorn moustache. Left arm is stiff from where one of his sex-mad breed bulls crushed him against the corral.'

Jim felt cold. 'The man I met was tall and skinny, with thin sandy hair.'

Bartells' eyes narrowed. 'Not Norton!'

'Well, there was that smell of gunsmoke when I arrived – just a hint, but no mistaking it. You think maybe this impostor and his crew jumped the real Norton, killed him and any men he had with him?'

The sheriff sat back in his chair, but close enough so he could rap his fingers against his desk edge. 'Funny you should say that.'

'You got a skewed sense of humour, Sheriff.'

'Mebbe.' He leaned forward, waved two yellow forms. 'Wires from the sheriff of Bisbee. And Mack Pendle.'

'Mack? Ella said in her wire she was sending a trail

crew, but wanted me to bring back the breeding records. I figured to tell you about Centavo, otherwise I would've likely met Mack and the crew on the desert trail.'

'And a sandstorm delayed you. Yeah, well, Mack wired to say he found five dead men in the barn at Norton's spread – sit down, dammit! I ain't through yet – five dead men in the barn, bodies mebbe coupla days old – and no herd.'

Allard slumped in his chair, head swimming. '*Five* dead men? There was only Norton and three others and I killed Centavo after he bushwhacked me. Doesn't make five.'

'Norton had four men working for him – had cut back his crew because he was selling-up, going back East to get married. That's the *real* Norton I'm talkin' about.'

'Then who was the feller I bought the herd from?'

'The one who killed Norton and his crew "sold" you the herd and not only made an extra ten thousand, but rustled the damn cows as well. He'll make even more down in Mexico.' Bartells sounded bitterly angry. 'Son of a *bitch*!'

Allard sat back to take it in, going over what the sheriff had said – and what he hadn't said. Suddenly he felt his hands gripping the arms of the chair tightly. His gaze bounced off the lawman's hard-planed face.

'Wait a minute!' Jim stopped, unable to say more, not having sorted it out properly in his mind. But enough so that he knew his suspicions were right: Bartells was trying to tie him into the murders and rustling. 'By God, you're the orneriest lawman I've ever known, Bartells! Your middle name must be "Suspicious".'

'I'm paid to be suspicious and this sounds a lot like that deal Bumper Tole accused you of.'

'And on his deathbed cleared me, for Chris'sake.'

'Might've figured to do you one last favour. Now, you sit still! You even look like reaching for your gun, you're a dead man, Allard!' He dropped a hand below desk level and brought up a sawn-off shotgun, laying it on the desktop, hand close to the cut-down butt. 'I ain't only suspicious, I'm damn careful, too.'

Allard kept his hands in his lap where they could be seen. 'How the hell would I have worked anything like this? Judas priest, I could've just wired Ella and had her give the bank authority to pay over the money in cash. . . .'

Bartells smiled slowly. 'Ain't that just what you done?'

'Dammit, I did it for this sonuver I believed was Norton, but I did think it strange he didn't come into the bank with me himself. The banker was leery, too, but Birch had authority to sell the herd and that seemed to satisfy him.'

'Way I figure it, you been riding the owlhoot more than once. An' Jubal Clay was no angel. You knew him and could've knowed this Norton impostor, worked it between you.'

'And then he sent Centavo after me? Why would he?'

'Save one share – either way it'd work. You kill Centavo, saves a share. He kills you . . .' Bartells spread his hands but quickly dropped his right to the shotgun again.

'Well, I guess that'd work – *if* I was in on it, which I wasn't.'

'And of which I ain't yet convinced. It's been done before. Someone checks out a herd for a prospective buyer, gives the OK, says the seller demands cash or the herd goes to someone else; money's wired through and the checker, the "seller", the cash and the whole damn herd all disappear.'

Jim had heard of such things: it wasn't even uncommon and had been tried in almost every cattle-raising State in the Union at one time or another.

'How about Purvis-Dalgetty? They know my reputation.'

Bartells's cold stare wavered very slightly but only for a fraction of a second. 'They go by word-of-mouth: I go by your actions – and you ain't what I'd call a non-violent man, Allard. Nor one who don't know his way around cattle country.'

'Damn you, Bartells! I can see where this is going and I want to punch you senseless so bad, I—'

'Don't.' The shotgun was in both hands now, hammers back, the professionally-shortened barrels yawning at Allard. 'I ain't a man who likes killin', but if it has to be done, I'll do it. Now shuck your gunbelt and come along to the cells.'

'I damn well knew it!' Jim gritted tossing his gunbelt on to the desk, the sudden movement making the sheriff jump and lift the gun. Allard tensed: he would have to watch his movements around this blamed lawman. He was jumpy – remembering that Allard had killed Jubal Clay, however he had done it. Jim knew it was only a quick way to Hell, tackling a man in that state while he held a sawn-off shotgun.

'Ella's on her way in,' the sheriff told him, as he locked a barred door. 'She dunno you're here yet but she'll find out soon enough.'

She arrived mid-afternoon and Allard was mighty irritable. He was still gritty and dirty from the sandstorm and Bartells had allowed him only one drink of water. Hannibal Hayes was the deputy on guard but the man dozed most of the time and refused to talk or bring him more water.

'Give me all the details, Jim,' Ella said, standing at the bars, Hayes lounging in the chair beside her, nursing his carbine. 'They don't seem to trust you very much.'

'They don't matter – do you trust me?'

She met his gaze squarely. 'As I said, give me the details, Jim. All of them.'

Allard did and she was very pale and quiet when he finished. He had noticed about halfway through, when he got to the part about meeting 'Norton', how she had tensed-up.

'You know something,' he said, when she didn't speak right away.

Ella nodded. 'The man who said he was Beau Norton – you say one of his men called him Wendell?'

'Well, that's what he yelled through the front door

70

and this ranny came out, said he was Norton.'

'He's Wendell Jones – my ex-husband.'

Jim got off his bunk and walked slowly across the cell to the door. 'You know, I mentioned the desert crossing and your name and he said, 'She's a bitch, ain't she?' and I had the queerest feeling he meant you and not the desert.'

She smiled thinly. 'That's Wendell. I won't go into the sordid details of our break-up. It's enough to say that once I was certain he was stealing what little money I had and was riding with outlaws on his trips away, I told him it was all over. We had a small ranch and I found he'd mortgaged it to the hilt, left me with big debts. I went all the way, charged him with theft and fraud. He got six months in Yuma. I haven't heard from him for more than a year – thank God, but he's a man who holds a grudge.'

'You figure this was all aimed at you?'

'You've every right to sound sceptical, but, yes, I do. Norton's ranch as you know is isolated. He had a small, experienced crew for his cross-breeding programme and there was no real reason for him to want to sell when he was having such success. That's why I was so eager to buy: it was just the right time for me. Almost pre-ordained, I thought, foolishly.'

'So Jones moved in, took over Norton's and . . . what? Waited for you to get word about the sale of the bulls?'

'Oh, no, Wendell isn't that random. I received a telegram, supposedly from Purvis-Dalgetty, advising me that Norton was selling and if I was interested I should put in my bid promptly and, of course, I expressed my interest right away with a wire to Norton. Just days before you arrived. And it was like – well, like it was meant to be, a man with your knowledge about such things turning up just then.'

'Bet Jones wasn't expecting that. I guess he saw I had suspicions, but I put them aside because I didn't want you to miss out on those bulls.'

She held up a hand. 'I know, Jim. Jake Bartells probably knows it, too, but is too hard-nosed to admit it. I'll explain to him and you'll soon be free again.'

It wasn't quite that easy; Ella had to threaten to bring in a lawyer before Bartells finally agreed to release Allard. 'You're still responsible for him, Ella. You keep a damn close eye on him.' It was a surly order and he now seemed anxious to be rid of them, even held the door open.

Out on the street again, Jim asked, 'Am I still working for you? I mean, I've just cost you ten thousand bucks you can't really afford.'

She paused and faced him. 'I borrowed that money in good faith and I bought that herd with it, so, I'm going to get back what's mine.'

'You're . . . what?'

'I'm going after the herd. And you're coming with me, Jim.'

'Hell, I'll go after the herd for you, feel obligated to do that anyway, but you can't—'

'Who says I can't? They're my cattle. I've paid for them and have committed myself to years of debt. I have to get them back, Jim, have to.'

He understood. There was just one thing that puzzled him: *how did Wendell Jones know Ella was inter-*

ested in that particular herd? And that she needed those
bulls to make her own breeding programme viable?

Mack Pendle had taken three men with him to help
drive the herd back to Panhandle: Arnie Bennett, a
wrangler named Kelty, and a big surly ranny whose
name Jim had forgotten: Cass someone, he thought.

They were waiting idly at Norton's place, lounging
about the house, had trashed some of the rooms
looking for whatever they might use. Mostly liquor.
They were all bleary-eyed when Allard and the girl
arrived, desert-worn and in no mood for the stupid
half-drunk antics of these cowpokes.

They weren't acting any different to any other
cowboys who had been thrust into the same situa-
tion, but one of them, Cass Cantrell, was an ugly
drunk and had a bigger snootful than the others who
tended more towards sleepiness or childish pranks.

Cantrell was a rawboned ranny, range-toughened,
and he not only leered at Ella when she spoke
sharply to him, but it was obvious he was mentally
undressing her: *likker-fired desire*, was what Allard
silently called it.

'What was we s'posed to do?' Cantrell demanded
cockily. 'We rid our asses raw crossin' that desert,
find all them dead men, then Mack lights out an' says
"wait". An' he also said, "help yourself to whatever
you want".'

'Generous of him,' Allard said. 'Where's he gone?'

'After the herd, he said.' Cantrell spoke sullenly,
reluctantly shifting his hot gaze to the drifter.

'Didn't the Bisbee sheriff arrange a posse to do

that after Mack called him out to see the bodies?' Ella asked, and Cass smiled and gave her his full lecherous attention.

'Guess so – Mack said he'd handle that part.' His smile disappeared. 'After givin' us the chore of diggin' graves.' He gestured to the five low mounds of fresh-turned earth in a small grove of trees away from the house. 'I tell you, ma'am, we earned our reward.' He belched and almost embarrassedly touched a hand to his mouth. 'Par'me!'

She glanced at Allard. He nodded briefly. 'Be mighty hot work.'

'All right. You three dip your heads in the horse trough or something and sober up. You can return to Panhandle. There's still plenty of work waiting to be done.'

The trio moaned and Cantrell, the eager spokesman, said, 'Hey! Them cows're on their way to Mexico. Ain't been there in a coon's age – we'll come with you.'

'You heard Mrs Jones.'

'Stay outa this, drifter. You're too new here to have a say in anythin'.'

Cantrell was turning nasty, dropped a threatening hand to his gun butt. Jim suddenly stepped forward, his six-gun coming up and whipping the tall ranny twice across the head, knocking his hat flying. Cass Cantrell stood there swaying, blinking, and then his legs folded like a squeeze-box and he spread out on his face in the dirt. One of the of other men, Kelty, shouted, 'Hey!' and lunged for Allard.

Jim clipped him with his gun barrel, too and Kelty

sat down, howling, holding his head. When Jim glanced at Bennett, the cowboy held up his hands, palms outwards, shaking his head, backing off.

'Drag 'em to the horse trough and dunk 'em. You find any tracks of the herd at all?'

'Mack did. Said they're headed for the Border.'

'That's a safe bet.'

They looked through the disordered house while the trio got their act together but found little – until Jim pulled out the middle drawer of a scarred old roll-top desk and it came all the way, spilling papers. He swore softly, stuffed them back in, but the drawer wouldn't close properly. Some more papers had fallen down the back, jamming it.

Amongst them he found a letter to Norton from a rancho he knew was outside Magdalena. He showed it to Ella.

'Ramon d'Angelo – I know of him. He's a cattle breeder, but leans mostly to Spanish stock. Though I did hear a whisper he was looking into crossing his herd with strong American cattle that would be tick-resistant.'

'Your rival for Norton's herd?'

She nodded, still reading. 'There's Norton's reply pinned on the back. He's willing to sell, but says he has given his word that I have first preference.'

'An honest man.'

'That was his reputation. He didn't deserve to end his life the way he did.'

She re-read the letters and Allard waited. When she glanced up, she seemed startled to see him watching her.

'How loyal is Mack Pendle?'

Ella frowned. 'Mack? Oh, he's a good ramrod. Loyal as anyone in that position, perhaps a trifle more so than most.'

'Because your father more or less raised him?'

She stiffened. 'Where did you get that idea?'

'Mack told me out on the range when I first arrived. Was warning me "not to get any smart ideas" – whatever he thought that meant.'

Her frown was deeply creased into her otherwise smooth forehead. 'Mack's worked for me for the past six or seven months. My father died long before that and they never met. Why would he say such a thing?'

Jim shrugged. 'Adding weight to his position, inferring he had your backing, I guess. Letting me know he could come down mighty hard if he figured he had to. He was leery of me right from the start – maybe because I knew something about cattle breeding. And I could have you spending a lot of your money.'

'Why would that bother Mack Pendle?'

'If he was in on the swindle with Norton's herd, he wouldn't want you spending money Jones was trying to cheat you out of. Cut down on everyone's share.'

She drew down a sudden deep breath. 'My God! You mean he could've helped Wendell set up this thing?'

'Did he know Jones?'

'Not as far as I know, but Mack was always kind of hungry for money, penny-pinching, even. Maybe he didn't know Wendell but if he was approached with a good enough offer—'

'He'd swing it. Yeah, I'll go along with that.'

She lifted a finger and thoughtfully tapped the air as she spoke. 'You know, he did encourage me to go after Norton's herd when I got that wire ... I should've wondered about that, but I was so excited to have the chance at such a good herd, I just jumped at it.'

'Well, I reckon if we pick up Pendle's tracks, he'll lead us to the herd. He'll be wanting his cut from Jones for whatever he did.' Jim paused, adjusting his words. 'I mean *I'll* pick up his tracks and go after the herd.'

'You can't do that alone, Jim.'

'Well, these three beauties won't be any help and don't think I'd trust 'em anyway.'

'When are you going to listen to me? Really *listen*, I mean? This ... is ... my ... herd! I've been cheated and the Clays have never stood still for being put-upon. So, *we*'ll head for the Border and follow Mack Pendle all the way to Magdalena if we have to.'

'It won't be the regular trail,' he said, making one last try to deter her. 'It'll be through some of the roughest, bandit-ridden country south of the Border. There'll be danger every foot of the way, Ella.'

She turned her face up to him, teeth bared in a deliberate caricature of a forced smile.

'It sounds wonderful. Let's get started.'

CHAPTER 7

TWISTED TRAIL

Jim Allard knew the country and he was mighty uneasy at the prospect of the girl's company.

This was probably the most lawless part of northern Mexico, riddled with *bandidos* and *rebeldes,* most of whom hated *gringos* – except American women: they tended to like, keeping them around their camps and using them as they saw fit. If they were too rebellious, well a swift slash with a *cuchillo* across the throat ended that – and there would be plenty of replacements. All they had to do was ride out and watch the trails south from the Border.

So he rode with his rifle across his thighs and he saw Ella's face once or twice, off-guard, as she looked around nervously, gaze jerking from shadow to shadow on the broken rockface of the desiccated country.

'You want to change your mind, I know someone in Santa Mercado who can escort you north.'

'I will not be changing my mind, Jim, so just forget any ideas along those lines.'

No use arguing, so he didn't give it another thought – concentrated now on getting them *both* safely through this corner of hell.

He dropped back a few times, keeping to the deep shadows of narrow passes through jagged, rearing slabs of rock thrown up by volcanic action in ancient times. Twice he climbed these, keeping the sloping face between him and the backtrail. He thought he detected some faint dust in the air, way back, but there was a hot wind blowing in desultory gusts so it was likely only a dust devil awakened briefly.

She waited for him patiently each time.

'Go easy on the water,' he told her as she corked her saddle canteen: he could hear it sloshing around so knew she had used more than half – in just one day, when they could have a week without sighting another waterhole or Indian well.

'My tongue seems too large for my mouth.'

'Suck one of them beads you got on a string round your neck. It'll help.'

'Break the necklace, you mean?'

'Not if it means more to you than staying alive.'

She flushed, though it was hard to be sure, with her face coloured up by the heat and the scorching sun. 'You're a hard man, aren't you, Jim? And . . . I notice when you fight you seem to – to retaliate very violently.'

'You want to win, you give back twice what you get. Some ranny hits you with a haymaker right, you give him one in the belly, several straight lefts, then tear his head off with your right. Keeps you on the right track.'

After a few moments she said, 'You've had a tough life, I think, Jim Allard.'

'It *is* a tough life out here. You have to adapt. You don't like it, you're gonna have one helluva time – or go under.'

'Your rules: do they apply to guns?'

'You mean, trade two bullets for one? Sure, why not? Long as you've got the ammunition, but don't do it just for the hell of it. Make it count.'

She was silent then as they made their way through tangled, rock-studded hills with dry brush dotting the parched landscape. He realized belatedly she had been asking him if that was how he had come to kill Jubal Clay: fanning his gun in retaliation to Clay's bullet tearing through his upper body. *Fact was, he didn't know! He had reacted instinctively and, in the end, he likely had done Clay a favour, but she was his sister and must wonder about it. . . .*

He swore silently for his careless answer to her question.

She rode in silence, slightly to one side. Twice he caught her angling her gaze at him. *Did she now see Clay's death as having been avoidable?*

Then, a couple of hours later, he turned sharply left without any warning. Ella frowned, followed, looked ahead and saw a smudge sliding across the sky. *Birds. Homing to evening water and Allard had seen them long before she did.*

Before sundown, they reached a small waterhole within a circle or rocks, the air alive with bird song and chatter. A few nervous, rodent-like animals were also drinking but swiftly disappeared into the heavier shadows as the pair rode in.

'This is our camp-site, I take it?'

He shook his head, pointed to the slope of a nearby ridge. 'Up there. No fire.'

For the first time she felt a real surge of fear.

'You think we're being followed?'

'Why risk it?'

Why indeed?

It wasn't yet daylight when Allard opened his eyes. He was huddled in his bedroll against some rocks and under a slight overhang. The girl was a few feet away in a more secure position that offered better protection in the event of attack.

The night had been cold as it always is in desert country and his hands were a little numb as he eased out of the blanket, bringing his rifle with him. The metal was warm from his body heat and he took the weapon with him behind a rock while he relieved himself. The girl hadn't stirred when he went back. He rolled up his blankets, knelt to undo the flap on a saddle-bag that contained hardtack. It would be a cold breakfast and he knew she wouldn't be happy about that after having put up with a cold, tasteless supper.

But it was a precaution he aimed to take, whether she liked it or not. It was the only thing that made sense in the circumstances and—

He froze, waxed-paper-wrapped cold meat half withdrawn from the bag's opening. He scarcely breathed as he cocked an ear.

Yeah! A horse and not one of theirs that were still hobbled between the rocks.

He reached down for the rifle and, still hunkered, crab-walked behind the flat rock, turning to face the direction of the sound even as the bay whickered softly, having heard the newcomer.

Jim had a shell already in the breech and eased back the hammer, glancing once towards the sleeping girl, then swung his gaze back to watch the deep shadow cast across the only decent way up. The horse there was coming, slowly, wearily – carefully.

He saw it: a glimpse of black mane, then a reddish head and he already had an idea of the owner. But the owner wasn't in the saddle: the horse was riderless.

Jim swung about, towards the rocks behind and to his left. If anyone was coming they would need to clamber over those and—

'Hold it, Allard! I got a twitchy finger!'

It was a warning which he heeded, but it was also said gaspingly: whoever it was, was hurt. 'You, Cantrell?'

'Judas! How you – pick me?'

'You hurt?'

'Yeah. Busted arm – twisted ankle – scalp crease.'

'Better come in – I'm laying down my rifle.'

'Colt – too. I know about you nailin' Jubal Clay.'

'Fluke, Cass. C'mon, man. You sound like you're about to collapse.'

Hard on the words he heard the man's gun clatter and then the awkward, flopping sounds of a falling body.

By the time he had carried the semi-conscious

Cantrell back to the cleared area of the campsite, the girl was awake. He was glad to see she was kneeling with her carbine cocked and ready, although she looked mighty leery.

'Cass Cantrell! What's he doing here?'

'Looks like he fell off a cliff after taking a bullet across the scalp.'

Putting crude splints on the arm and wrapping them around with a length of rope, brought Cantrell awake, cussing a blue streak. The girl gave him a drink from her canteen as much to shut him up as to slake the thirst she knew he must be suffering. She had wiped most of the dried blood and dirt from his face, bandaged his head roughly.

He looked up and nodded his thanks, swivelled his gaze to the waiting Allard who had unsaddled Cantrell's mount and given it a cupful of water out of his hat. Jim's rifle was within reach all the time.

'I . . . think I shook him. Fluke I found you – was the hoss, my work-mount – woulda scented your bay – an' your claybank, ma'am.'

'What happened?' Allard's voice was hard. 'Don't start in the middle.'

Cantrell's eyes showed a shade of resentment at the tone but he was in a lot of pain and, in his own rough way, grateful for the splint on his arm and the support bandage on his ankle. The scalp wound was giving him a pounding headache.

'After you went, we found some more likker in Norton's house,' he slurred, lowering his gaze, but neither Jim nor Ella said anything.'We drank our supper. . . .'

The trio became boisterous, Arnie Bennett challenging Kelty the wrangler to 'break him in'.

'Bet you cain't ride me bare-back – no damn spurs, though! – an' bring me to a standstill!' slurred Bennett. 'Bet I can throw you, show you up for the lousy bronc-buster you are.'

'I'll ride you into the goddamn ground!' Kelty swore, the whiskey talking.

Cass Cantrell urged them on: he could do with some entertainment.

Bennett took one more long swig, wiped his mouth with the back of his hand and got down on all fours. 'OK, climb aboard an' pick yo'self a soft patch to land on!'

'When I land, it'll be on top of you when you fall flat on your ugly face!'

'Ride 'im, cowboy!' Cantrell yelled owlishly.

Then Kelty only pretended to remove his spurs, straddled Bennett's broad back and twisted one hand in the loose folds of the man's filthy shirt. Instantly Bennett let out a fair imitation of a whinnying mustang and began bucking and swaying, scampering over the thin grass, jerking his body side to side, arching his back, rearing up.

Kelty held on tightly, his free arm rising and falling, slapping the air as he would if riding a real wild mustang. Then, when the sweating Bennett dropped back to all fours, he raked the man's thighs with his spurs.

This brought a roar of pain and instant, indignant

cursing from Bennett. He tried to fling Kelty off, no longer pretending to be a horse, standing, staggering under Kelty's weight, reaching around awkwardly to throw the man.

Cantrell was doubled up with laughter as the two men staggered and lurched around the yard in front of Norton's ranch house.

Then a rifle cracked twice from out of the darkness and Kelty was hurled away from Bennett who staggered and awkwardly stumbled to all fours again. Kelty's body hit limply in that certain way that told the shocked, drunken Cantrell the man was dead before he hit the ground.

Cantrell began to run, blindly, across the yard, towards and beyond the corrals. He fell, rose, stumbled again, cannoned a shoulder off a nubbing-post. The rifle whiplashed twice, then in a short volley of three. He heard bullets tear a path through the night, glanced back, and saw Bennett sprawled on the ground.

A bullet took his hat off and he stumbled, put down a hand to right himself, and kept on running. There was a slope here and his legs had trouble keeping up with his momentum: *goddamn firewater!* If ever there was a time he wished to be stone cold sober!

He fell, rolling and skidding, beginning to yell as he realized he was heading for the lip of a steep drop above one of the ancient dry washes where Norton had kept some of his herd. He fought and kicked, trying to slow his pace, reared up from the waist as he managed to snatch at a bush, but the rough bark ripped at his palm. Then his head snapped back amidst a swirl of bright lights and he fell away into the darkness below. . . .

'Son of a bitch must've figured he'd killed me,' he ended his story. 'Guess I thought so, too! But I came round with my arm jammed under me and hurtin' like hell, an' what I figured was a busted ankle. Dunno how I climbed out, but I made it an' got a hoss from the corral. No one around by then an' Kelty an' Bennett were both dead.'

Ella was watching Jim who asked, 'See who it was?'

Cantrell stared at them both. 'You – you ain't gonna b'lieve me.'

'Let's hear it.'

Cantrell was still reluctant, licked his lips but Allard put his hand on the canteen and shook his head. Cass scowled then took a deep breath.

'I didn't see him clear – just an outline – but I know it well enough.' Another pause until he saw Jim's face hardening with impatience and he added with a rush, 'Was Jake Bartells.'

Both the girl and Allard were silent, stunned. 'You must be mistaken, Cass!'

'No, ma'am.'

'You were drunk, head-shot, and had fallen off a cliff. Not a reliable witness, Cantrell.'

Cantrell was rousing some now, and his face showed his anger at their scepticism.

'Told you you wouldn't believe me, but I seen him well enough! I seen his hoss that he rides, too. An' that damn tall hat is a dead giveaway.'

'Anyone can buy a hat like that in Godfrey's,' Jim

pointed out and Cantrell scowled.

'Jim, I think we have to believe Cass.'

Allard thought so, too, privately. But – it took some swallowing.

What the hell was the sheriff up to? Did he mistake Bennett and Kelty and Cantrell for some of Jones's crew? *Not likely.*

Even in the dark he ought to know local cowboys.

'What's Bartells playing at, Ella?'

She shook her head. 'Whatever it is, I-I don't like the way things are shaping up, Jim.'

Nor did he.

This was a twist in the trail he hadn't counted on.

CHAPTER 8

BADGE-TOTER

Cass Cantrell passed out again before they were ready to leave. His legs simply folded under him in mid-sentence and he crashed to the dust, limp as wet laundry.

'What're we going to do with him?' asked the girl anxiously. 'His head wound's bleeding again.'

'Not fit to travel. Have to leave him.'

She looked aghast. 'You can't do that! Not in this country.'

'What's the choice? Make a travois, hitch it to his roan and let him slow us down?'

'Jim, I said earlier you're a hard man, but this is too . . . too extreme! A wounded man! He can't fend for himself with a broken arm and his ankle swollen to twice its normal size. Even if we left him food and water—'

'Which we can't afford to.'

'Even if we left him some, how long could he last?

There's no chance of help coming along here. It's too far back to the Border and Bisbee.' Suddenly her face lit up as she swung her gaze to him. 'You said you know someone in Santa Mercado; couldn't they take care of him?'

'Someone like you, not some wild-eyed cowboy who's on his way down to being a saloon swamper – if he can stay sober long enough to push a broom.'

Her eyes narrowed and her hands planted on her hips. 'You are *miserable*, Jim Allard! You know that?'

'Do now.'

'Oh, don't be so – so damn smart! Look, I'm your boss and you're supposed to do what I say. *Supposed* to! And I say this: we take Cass to Santa Mercado and then continue after the herd.'

'Gonna lose a helluva lot of time. Thought you felt stronger about them cows than that.'

'I feel strongly about leaving a wounded man who's worked for me for almost a year, and has been no better and no worse than the usual run of ranch hands. Will you lead us there?'

He was reluctant: Jones was already way ahead of them. Bartells – if that's who it was killed Kelty and Bennett – would be somewhere ahead, too, if they made the detour, an added danger now and, so far, an unknown one. It wasn't clear what part the sheriff played in this so it was anybody's guess just what he might or might not do.

'Santa Mecardo's a day's ride, at least.'

She gestured to the pale light, the sun-up colours fading slowly. 'It's early yet.'

That small jaw jutted determinedly and the feet

were planted firmly. He saw the futility of arguing further.

'Let's get started.'

There wasn't much wood available to build a proper travois, everything was way too short. So he bound four pieces together into two longer shafts, secured the apex with two cross-bars, and two more towards the base.

'Won't be very comfortable but guess Cantrell won't mind.'

She threw him a hard look. She was kneeling beside the semi-conscious Cantrell, mopping his beet-red face with a dampened cloth.

'Don't waste that moisture. Dribble it across his lips. Into his mouth would be better.'

Ella wrinkled her nose, started to disagree, but realized it was a sensible suggestion. Cantrell's tongue tip made several probing journeys across his scaled lips and when Jim lifted him on to the travois, now spread with blankets, Cass opened his eyes.

'I ... owe ... you,' he gasped, looking up into Allard's face.

'Not me. Her. I'd as soon leave you.'

'Ex-expected you to.'

They got under way, Cantrell falling quiet, moaning once or twice. Ella held back when they came to the bottom of an obviously rugged, rocky slope with splintered slabs leaning at odd angles across what trail there was. Her horse was restless, sensing they were going to cross this dangerous place.

'Can't we go round?'

'Never been round, but I'd say it'd add another

day. This is a long spur. . . . Wouldn't be near as hard without the travois.'

Her mouth tightened and she spurred her horse forward and up by way of answer.

Jim might have smiled a little, but he kept it to himself, leaned from the saddle and rapped the roan to get it moving. He was glad he was saddle-borne and not in that contraption, jarring and rocking and scraping along.

They almost lost Cantrell twice, the travois tilting dangerously, the roped joins beginning to sag. The man had passed out again so was mercifully unaware of his danger.

Going down was almost as risky, Allard choosing a straight descent to save twisting the assembly any more than necessary by riding zigzag-fashion.

They had glimpsed the scattered adobe buildings of Santa Mercado and, though he didn't mention it, Jim had seen several shadowy riders in the rocks lining the trail winding across the flats to the town. He gave the roan's lead reins to the girl and unshipped his rifle, saying nothing.

She tensed when he rode on ahead, obviously very alert.

They made the town as the sun was setting, a few Mexicans and a scattering of *gringos* watching them from ragged *galerias*, or window spaces, some showing wind-tattered curtains, others just blank, empty of any kind of screening.

Not a church in sight – nor any saints, either.

But she wasn't worried about how the town was named: her horse had spotted the water trough under a lone tree halfway along the street where it widened into a small, shadeless plaza. It began to act-up and she fought it stubbornly. 'I don't care for this place, Jim!'

'You ought to see the sleazy side – fact, you will.'

'Is – is that where your friend is?'

He nodded. 'If she's in town.'

'She?'

'Yeah. *Cantina* gal. One of them you read about in dime romance novels – good-time gal with a heart of gold.'

'I think you're making fun of me.'

His eyebrows arched innocently. 'It's true.'

It was. Her name was Felicity and she was a woman in her early forties and must have had many men fighting over her when she was younger. She was still a fine-looking woman, her figure enlarged a little, but she had a pleasant face and an infectious laugh that opened her red mouth wide.

'Your *amigo* has what we call *commoción* – er – *cerebral?*'

'Concussion. Yeah, Felicity, and he's not my *amigo*.' Her big dark eyes slid to Ella, then back to Allard, registering a query. He smiled, shaking his head. 'Nor hers. Just a man who works on her ranch.'

She nodded slowly, unwinding the head bandage carefully, bringing a groan or two from Cantrell. 'Ah, *sí*. This I can fix – but not very soon. A few days, perhaps.'

'We'll be gone by morning.'

The Mexican woman glanced at Ella and then wiggled her eyebrows at Jim, but he laughed briefly, shaking his head again. 'I'll sleep in your store-room.'

She gusted a hearty laugh and slapped him on the shoulder. '*Antiguo*!'

He laughed and said something in rapid Spanish that stopped her laughter and the look she flung at Ella seemed to have a little more respect in it. 'Ah – *siiiiii*!'

Next morning, riding away from the dreary scattering of buildings in a light mist, the air cool, Ella put her claybank alongside his bay and said, 'Why does she agree to look after Cantrell?'

'Because I asked her to.'

'That's what I mean, Jim. Why does she agree to take care of a gunshot stranger just because you ask her to?'

'Long story.'

She gestured ahead with her quirt, indicating the long flats giving way to grey dunes that already had small plumes of sand blowing from their crests. 'It's a long ride.'

He sighed. 'I got her husband out of some trouble once – when she had a husband.'

She waited. 'Is that all?'

'That's my answer.'

'Oh. What did you say to her last night when she accused you of getting old?' She laughed at his surprise. 'I understand some Spanish, but you spoke too quickly for me.'

He shrugged. 'I agreed I might be getting old, but, if I felt *too* old in the same bed as you, I'd probably blow my brains out.'

She stiffened in the saddle, face flushing furiously. 'I should've expected something like that. It was a bawdy laugh she gave, but then she's a bawdy woman, isn't she?'

'That kinda remark don't suit you, Ella.'

She flushed more deeply if anything, fiddled with the reins. 'No. I-I guess I didn't mean it. In fact, I suppose I should thank you for the compliment.'

'Por nada.'

'Oh, don't cheapen it!'

He said nothing and then, deliberately changing the subject, she said, 'I saw you talking with Cass this morning. He seems better doesn't he?'

'More than that. He's grateful, believe it or not.'

Her head came up swiftly. 'He told you something?'

'Yeah. Says Mack Pendle offered every man working for Panhandle five dollars if they would tell him about any rustling they knew was going on in the area. Not just Panhandle stock, but anywhere around Pine County.'

'That's a strange thing to do.'

'Not if you're looking for someone who's good at throwing a wide loop – and want to do a deal with him Maybe even have some particular herd in mind, but need a pard.'

She thought about it. 'Trying to find an ally?'

'Sure. If he wasn't too sure of the country himself. Or the best way to get a bunch of rustled critters across the Border. Or if he knew those things but needed someone to get some cows together while he stayed on as ramrod.'

'Well, I'll be damned!' she said. 'I never suspected anything. But I never lost any more than the usual odd steer. I made sure my breeding herd was always well guarded. I'm sure rustlers didn't bother us.'

'Mack seems to've been after bigger things – like getting himself a pardner like Jones. And the kind of deal Jones pulled with Norton. He's been biding his time, is my guess. Maybe he helped Jones set up this deal, telling him about your finances and so on. Or maybe he came in a little late and has decided that Jones has done the hard work, now all he has to do is go in and take the money off him.'

They rode without speaking for some time until they started into the first low sandhills.

'Yes, I think maybe Mack Pendle is capable of doing those things,' she said abruptly. 'But he's a very tough and obviously a mighty patient man, waiting all this time!'

'Could be he caught a whisper and just sat back to watch developments.' He steadied his gaze on her expectant face. 'That's a heap of money he's set his sights on. Worth waiting – or killing – for.'

'Yes, and I believe he *is* capable of killing for it.'

Jim nodded. 'Just so you know.'

'I'm not afraid, Jim Allard! I keep telling you that. It's my herd I've paid for it with money I have to earn and repay the bank. Which I fully intend to do. If some of the thieves have to . . . die . . . along the way, then so be it.'

She tilted that small, firm jaw at him and, carefully smothering a smile he felt tugging at his lips, he said, 'And you reckon *I'm* a hardcase.'

Ella's resolve was tested soon afterwards.

They were riding through a cutting on the far side of the sandhills, almost across this desolate section, when Ella's claybank suddenly jerked its head violently, starting a whinny, drowned by the gunshot. It began to fall and the mouth was already red-tinged, even as the girl cried out and threw herself from the saddle, wriggling to cover.

Allard wrenched the head of his bay around swiftly, leaned down and snatched the lead-rope of the pack horse and ran his mount behind some jutting, weather-hardened slabs of sand. They had compacted long ago and when the ceaseless hot winds had blown away the loose sand, the shapes of embryo boulders had remained.

The rifle triggered again, two quick shots, followed by a pause and another that put a bullet through the canvas covers on the pack-saddle, causing the horse to lurch violently and whinny. But the animal itself wasn't hit and Jim released the rope, allowed it to run on into the cutting.

His rifle slid from the scabbard as he dived off the bay, hit rolling, and slewed his lean body in behind the slim protection offered. The bay followed the pack horse and Allard, watching a drift of gunsmoke on top of a dune, saw part of a man's leg showing as he rose to shoot at the horse.

Allard's Winchester jarred against his shoulder, the lever worked with a gritty sound, and his second bullet either made the gunman up there duck, or else struck him and he dropped below the curve of the crest.

For good measure, Jim put three more shots along the crest, sand spurting. Then he was moving, crouching, running from the temporary shelter to the base of the dune. He kept moving to the right, where the dune's slopes lowered, waiting for lead to slam into him or zip into the sand around his pounding boots.

The gun up top fired a fast volley, but the shots were directed at the slabs. *Good! The son of a bitch hadn't seen him leave the shelter.*

He crossed the lowest part of the dune and started to climb up, working along the face a little, giving himself some shelter. He dropped flat, face pressed into the grey, coarse sand, spitting, blasting grit from his nostrils. The ground beneath him was loose and moving: lying prone, the sand was already sliding down and building against his body.

Not going to be any fun getting up there!

He had to do it, though, hoped the girl had enough sense to keep her head down, hide behind the claybank's carcass, maybe. Anyway, the killer was still shooting in his direction, or, where he thought Jim was hiding.

Allard thrust to his feet and started running up immediately, feeling the tearing strain clamp his leg muscles right from the start. His boots made a slight squeaking sound but that couldn't be avoided. He breathed through his mouth, lungs beginning to burn: *cowboys were meant to ride, not do this kind of running!*

He weaved, slipped twice, knew there was sand clogging the rifle barrel now. But he persevered, straining, hoping to get up there and behind the rifleman before he was seen. The killer was still shooting, but more slowly now, as if he was testing various positions, no longer sure his quarry was behind those jutting slabs.

Glancing up as he paused, one hand pressed against the mobile sand, Jim tried to settle his breathing. He groaned as he saw the shadow of the killer moving. The man was turning, finally checking his back – and he couldn't help but see Allard.

He saw him all right and, kneeling, lifted his rifle quickly to his shoulder. Jim threw himself across the slope, landing on his back, swinging the rifle one-handed and hoped the sand in the barrel wouldn't be enough to cause the breech to blow apart. It wasn't, but when the rifle fired it had much more recoil than usual and jumped from his grip. He snatched at the weapon as it slid into the sand, already half-covered. But even as he did, he saw the man up there, jerk and topple forward. The body came sliding and tumbling down. Jim floundered across to intercept it.

And the man came alive, apparently only winged. He twisted on to his back and drove both boots against Allard, sending him flying down the slope, rolling out of control, to the flatter area below. Jim grabbed at sand that went through his fingers like water, didn't slow his descent any at all.

The killer used his momentum to help him, dug in his heels and heaved upright, launched himself across, big hands reaching. Allard had a confused glimpse of the big body coming at him and then they were locked together, sliding the rest of the way on to the flatter, firmer sand below. He grunted, hooked an elbow into the side of the man's neck, and the head slid down almost under Jim's arm. He tried to get a grip but the head snapped up and caught him under the jaw, teeth clacking together solidly. Jim reeled and then big fists hammered at his face and upper body.

Blood flowed from his nose, his lips crushed against his teeth, his head rocked. He lifted a knee by instinct and caught the other man in the midriff, missing the more vulnerable genitals. But his opponent tried to protect himself there by instinct and dropped his hands.

Allard slammed a hammer blow into the side of his head, knocking the man's hat off and immediately recognizing Mack Pendle. The ramrod was tough, tried to rear up, and Jim kicked him in the chest, the impact sending Mack spinning. He rolled on to the flat sand. Allard jumped down beside him, kicked him in the head. Pendle rolled back and, dazed, dropped his hand towards his gun butt.

Jim went for his own gun and Mack gasped, 'Wait! Wait up!'

Allard drew smoothly, cocked the hammer, but didn't fire. Mack looked mighty relieved as he got to his knees, hands out to the side. Suddenly he groped inside his torn shirt.

'Don't be loco!' Allard gasped, thrusting his Colt forward. 'I'll blow your head off before you get that hideaway working!'

But Pendle swallowed, too winded to speak, brought his hand out, clasped around something that flashed metallically in the sun. *Derringer, Jim thought.* He pushed the hand towards the tensed Allard and opened his fingers.

No derringer: he was holding a badge.

Raised letters read: *Deputy US Marshal.*

CHAPTER 9

DESERT STORM

Allard lit the cigarette he had rolled for Mack Pendle and looked hard into the man's reddened eyes as he shook out the match.

'That's why you offered a bribe to cowhands at Panhandle to let you know about any rustling going on?'

'Except you. Didn't like you from the start. Somethin' about you, Allard. Too tough, too sure of yourself without struttin' like a prairie rooster, knew and saw a lot more'n you let on.'

Jim had nothing to say about that but Ella, sitting close by, nodded gently to herself: looked like she thought Pendle had summed-up Allard to her own way of thinking.

'Small change for an undercover marshal, catching the odd rustler, isn't it?'

Mack managed to grin though his mouth had been mashed by Jim's fist not long ago. 'Not just any

101

old rustler. I've been huntin' Wendell Jones for a long time and my boss said, "Go undercover and get the son of a bitch – no matter how long it takes".' He shrugged. 'He was in kind of a real tizzy at the time, bein' rid by politicians and so on, and I wasn't sure he meant it, but I took him at his word. Thought about Ella and – er – persuaded her ramrod to up and quit, but to recommend me as a replacement.'

'Did your *persuasion* include a beating?' Ella asked stiffly, and again Pendle shrugged. 'Because Simm had been beaten rather badly when he turned in the job.'

'He was paid well enough.'

'Why did you think Ella might lead you to Jones? They'd been divorced a couple of years and she'd put him in jail—' Jim stopped speaking, suddenly seeing it, nodded gently. 'Uh-*huh*. You knew him well enough to figure he wouldn't let her get away with sending him to Yuma, right?'

She sucked in a deep breath, frowning slightly in Allard's direction, then looked quickly at Mack Pendle.

'Yeah. He'd been lyin' low, but I heard a whisper he was gonna square with Ella, was workin' on a slick deal that'd let him do that, ruin her, and make him a heap of *dinero* all in one.'

Her teeth tugged lightly at her bottom lip. Jim thought some colour had gone out of her face. 'Almost a year!' she breathed. 'You worked for me all that time and never even hinted you were a lawman. Or that I might be in danger!'

'I was workin' mainly for the Marshals' Service,

ma'am. I kept sendin' reports in to headquarters that were kind of a little more optimistic than things actually were. But I was gatherin' information, could see where it was leadin'.'

'But still didn't think to warn me!'

'Aw, now, Ella, what good would that've done? I'd've tipped my hand and missed catchin' Jones. As it is, I'm damned mad you never sent me to Norton's in the first place, instead of Allard. I'd've been able to catch Jones red-handed.'

She looked from Pendle to Allard. 'You both seem to understand each other, but all I see is I've been used.'

'Not by me,' Jim said easily, a touch of defensiveness in his tone.

'Perhaps not, but, certainly by you, Mack!'

Pendle held up a hand. 'All part of my job, Ella. I can't say sorry because I'm not. It's put me within spittin' distance of Jones and this time I aim to get him, solid enough to watch him swing from the gallows.'

'He must've done something pretty damn big for it to be worth all this effort.'

Mack snorted and immediately clapped a hand lightly over his swollen nose. He spat to one side.

'Well, for one thing, it ain't the first time he's pulled this kind of a switch – only last time it was horses from a breeding and stud ranch.' He smiled briefly. 'Happened to belong to a senator . . . who had a nice young wife and an even nicer young daughter.' He flicked his eyes at the girl and said no more, seeing that Jim savvied his meaning.

But Ella was no fool – after all, she had once been married to Wendell Jones. 'He always was a womanizer. Looking back, I believe his infidelity may've even started on our honeymoon.'

'Maybe you're lucky: he killed the senator's wife.'

She frowned, shocked and horrified. Neither man said anything. She looked suddenly stubborn, then deliberately hardened her face. 'I want my herd back, Mack. I'm committed to repaying the money I've borrowed whatever happens, but I *want that herd*!'

'Last I know, he's still with it, but one contact told me he was planning on selling it off without the Hereford bull and the best Brahman. Keepin' 'em.'

Ella had stiffened. 'My God! He's not finished with me yet then!'

'No, ma'am.'

'Contacts – out here?'

Pendle's face was blank. 'I've been a long time workin' for the Marshals, Allard. Always careful, so I could come back and look up those who'd been helpful. Never failed me yet.'

'You've crossed this desert before then.' Pendle nodded curtly and Jim knew he wouldn't answer any more questions along those lines. So he changed tack. 'Since when does a US marshal, undercover or not, ambush a couple of ordinary folk?'

He was surprised how uncomfortable Pendle suddenly seemed. The man smoked his cigarette all the way down before he answered. 'Wasn't aimin' to kill nobody. Just meant to wing your claybank, Ella, but' – he gestured to his face – 'my eyes ain't so good. Small sandstorm hit last night. I got caught flat-footed. Near blinded me and by then I'd lost Jones and my water canteen. I figured to put you afoot – leavin' you the pack horse, mind – while I moved on and tried to make up lost time.'

'I suppose you were only going to wing my horse, too?'

After a long silence, Mack said, 'Was gonna wing *you*, not your hoss.'

'My God!' exclaimed the girl. 'And you're supposed to be a *lawman*!'

'Told you, I didn't like the look of Allard right from the start. I din' know what he was up to – still don't – but I figured he was gonna make money outa you some way.'

Jim's eyes were hard but he remained silent until Pendle shrugged once more.

'I mean, what kinda man would bother bringing a beat-up saddle with a silver plate worth maybe twenty bucks all the way to Casa Grande, just as a favour to a man he'd killed anyway?'

It was the girl who answered and it surprised Jim. 'He'd given his word to Jubal! His *word*! And he was man enough to want to honour it. Or can't you understand that?'

Mack looked amused. 'You got a lot to learn, lady.'

'I'm learning all the time!' the girl snapped. 'And what I've learned about you, Mack Pendle, does not please me very much at all.'

'That don't bother me – goes with the job.'

'How about Bartells?' Jim asked suddenly, making Pendle blink.

'Bartells?'

'Is he part of this deal?'

Mack frowned, thought about it, shook his head slowly. 'Not as far as I know.'

'He's cut loose. Killed Kelty and Bennett at Norton's, almost got Cass Cantrell, too. Bartells is out here somewhere.'

'Who's he trailin'? Jones or me?' No comment about the deaths of men he had lived and worked with.

'Don't you know?'

'Damned if I do. He don't know I'm a marshal. Leastways, don't think so. He must be after Jones.' He snapped his fingers suddenly. 'I must've missed Jake in that sandstorm. He'll be well ahead of us by now!'

'*Us?*'

'Well, all three of us are after Jones, ain't we? Might as well pool our resources.'

'And yours are. . . ?'

Mack grinned and fumbled out his badge, holding it for both to see. 'As a duly sworn officer of the United States Federal Marshal's Service, I hereby request and insist that you both, as good citizens of the said US, render me any or all assistance that I require. Now it's legal.'

'Not the first time you've used that ploy.'

Mack grinned crookedly. 'And won't be the last. What say we brew up some of that coffee I smell amongst your packs on that jughead and then get underway? We might even overtake Bartells.'

Or he might lie in wait to ambush us, thought Jim.

*

106

But Jake Bartells had troubles of his own.

The cursed sandstorm had gotten him turned around somehow and he was lost. It had been short and violent, a *rapido tormenta*, as they called these storms in this part of Mexico. Of short duration, it had yet changed the shape of landmarks and, not really at home in these southern wastelands, the sheriff had trouble returning to the old trail he had been following.

There had been someone between him and Jones, too, and he had been closing in when the storm struck out of the dusk, turning the night into impenetrable blackness. Even his mount seemed disoriented come morning. He was low on water, dry enough for his tongue to cling to the roof of his mouth by the time he saw familiar country in the distance, around mid-afternoon.

He swore. He was way too far south and east. Wrenching the head of his mount around hard enough to bring a whinny of protest from it, he suddenly paused.

A greyness yonder, backed by distant, broken ridges.

'Goddlemighty! That must be Mercado – Judas *priest*! I'm way, way too far off.'

But why not make use of the town, now he was this close? It was a long time since he had been there but last time – for a 'consideration' – he had ridden out and left a wanted *Americano bandido* to enjoy the comforts of a woman he had found to his liking. The man probably wasn't there now, maybe not even alive, but the woman would be. He knew a born survivor when he saw one and had a hunch Elena

Delgado, she of the big breasts, would still be in Santa Mercado.

He was right, and when he stepped into her shack she was just farewelling a customer who resented the intrusion. Foolishly, he lunged at Bartells with a short-bladed knife and a snarl. He died with that snarl still twisting his lips, Bartell's bullet through his heart at point-blank range. The wide-eyed woman hurriedly encased her main assets in her grimy blouse, ropy hair flying across her face as she backed up against the wall.

Bartells grinned: he knew no one in this dump would come to investigate the gunshots, even if they had been heard outside this remote shack.

'*Buenas dias, pecho*! You ain't got any skinnier since last time I was here.'

She recognized him then and her full lips trembled a little until she firmed them up and allowed the rouged smile to split her vixen-like face. 'Jake! Jake, *mio*! Oh, I thought you would never come back.'

She stepped up to him hands, reaching for his face, fingers ready to caress. One big hand encircled her slim wrists, clamping them like a manacle, and his grin widened as she rose to her toes, gasping in pain. He waved the smoking gun barrel under her small nose which she wrinkled and then sneezed.

He laughed out loud, swung her by the wrists and she stumbled over the corpse now still on the floor. She cowered as he advanced. 'Sorry to be so rough, *querida*, but I'm in a hurry, and need to know if any strangers have come to town or passed through lately. Start talkin'. Right now!'

Ten minutes later, he left the shack, ignoring the sounds of sobbing, and made for the house where he knew that snooty Felicity Damora lived. *For the moment, anyway. . . .*

He went quickly around the side of the house and the first thing he saw was Cass Cantrell taking his ease in a narrow bed set up on the shaded *galeria*.

The wounded man turned casually, then dropped his glass of tequila and lemon, twisting painfully under the sheet to grope for his six-gun. Bartells smiled crookedly and brought up his Colt, freezing Cass in mid-movement.

'No, *señor*!' cried Felicity, as she came on to the gallery, holding a switch broom. She ran forward and swung at Bartells who knocked her aside with one chunky fist. She fell, skidded on the flagstones, blood dribbling from her nose. Dazed, she sat there, weight supported on one arm.

The sheriff had Cass under the gun, ordered him to drop his Colt on the sheet at the end of the bed where he could see it. Cantrell obeyed, eyes wary beneath the bandage still swathed around his head.

'I should've made sure of you, Cass, took a look over that damn cliff.'

'You should've,' Cantrell agreed, not knowing what else to say.

The sheriff watched him carefully, occasionally giving a moment's attention to the still dazed woman. 'How'd you get here? You couldn't've been fit enough to ride.'

'I sprouted wings,' Cass said sullenly and then slammed back violently against the headboard as

Bartells shot him in the upper arm. The man groaned and fell on his side, blood soaking into the bedding.

Bartells whirled as Felicity came to her feet, swinging the broom. He punched her in the midriff and she fell, winded. He stood beside her, planted a boot across her contorted face, adding just a little warning pressure.

'Now, folks, you know no one's gonna come lookin' to see who's doin' the shootin'. Hereabouts they don't care to poke their nose in somethin' that ain't their business – 'less they want it shot off or mashed into their face. Like what could happen to you, *señorita*! Sooooo – seems like I got me a captive audience don't it?' He lifted his boot from her face.

'You will never leave here . . . alive!' Felicity gasped, wiping her bleeding nose on her apron. 'I have friends!'

Bartells laughed. 'Lady, when I leave, I'll take half the two-legged snakes who live here with me. I been kinda worried about tacklin' Jonesy all alone, but now I can get me some cheap labour. A handful of *pesos* oughta do it.'

'Not if I tell them how much money you're going after!' the woman said tightly.

Cass, through his pain, tried to signal her not to threaten this killer-lawman, but it was too late.

'Fact is, Felicity, you won't be able to tell no one anythin', nor will he. You'll die before I leave – but there's dyin' and *dyin'*.' He toed out a chair and dropped into it, still with that cold smile and the deadly look. 'So, why don't you bring me a glass of whatever Cass was drinkin' an' we'll talk about it – an' bring in that pretty l'il daughter of yours you keep hid away from the local scum. I'd like to see how she's growed, if she's gonna be as good-lookin' as you once were. Must be – what? Ten, eleven by now?'

Felicity felt so weak she could barely speak above a whisper. She clasped her hands in supplication as she faced the sheriff. '*Madre de Dios*! Oh, please, *señor*, do not hurt my Margarita. . . .'

Face like chiselled granite, Bartells flicked his gun barrel. '*Bring her here*! Then we'll talk, won't we?'

CHAPTER 10

SIGHTING

They had redistributed the load from the pack horse between the three of them. Allard was riding his bay, Mack Pendle had his roan and Ella took her saddle from the dead claybank and rode the pack horse. It was an older animal, a paint, one time cow pony, but now used to a plodding gait, so it virtually acted as a pacemaker, slowed them down considerably.

'Jones is gonna do his deal and be lost to hell an' gone by the time we catch up with him – if we ever do!' Pendle bitched, not for the first time.

'Your own fault for shooting Ella's horse.'

Pendle scowled, cast a brief look at the girl and was mildly surprised at the hostility in her dusty face.

'I won't forget that, Mack.'

He grunted and pulled on ahead again, unable to completely contain his impatience. Jim set his bay alongside the old paint.

112

'Want to try and lose him?'

Her head snapped around. 'Could we?'

He hesitated, looked around the open country they had to cross before they reached the broken, rugged greyness beyond. He sighed and shook his head.

'I guess not. Not here, leastways. Maybe when we get into those canyons. Be risky. He's got an itchy trigger finger, but he may not want to shoot, in case Jones and his men are still within earshot.'

Her mouth felt dry, and not just because their water was strictly rationed. 'We – we better see what chances offer themselves.'

Jim nodded, squinting, scanning the shadowed upheaval of shattered volcanic rocks dancing in the heat-haze. *Be one helluva place to get lost in; besides, they could use Mack's gun if and when they confronted Jones.*

The girl had the right idea: wait and see.

When they were a mile closer, Jim Allard lifted his mount to a small rise, shaded his aching, gritty eyes, and studied that slice of hell waiting out there for them to cross.

The girl rode up alongside, obviously curious. Pendle, ahead by a hundred yards hipped in his saddle and when he saw Allard, stood in the stirrups. 'Come on!'

Allard held up a hand in a gesture that could have been a wave of acknowledgement, or a sign for Pendle to wait-up.

'What is it, Jim?' The girl was standing up to the gruelling ride pretty well, but her voice was hoarse, her lips dry and scaled.

'That country – does Jones know much about cattle?'

'Ye-es, I suppose you could say he does. Mostly learned from rustling, I guess, but he could've made a good rancher if he'd set his mind to it. But he's restless and impatient to be rich . . . why?'

Allard didn't answer, set his horse down the slope past the girl and, frowning, she turned and heeled the slow old paint after him.

Mack Pendle was sitting his mount, body stiff with impatience, hands folded on the saddlehorn. 'What's up?'

'You had a good look at that country up ahead?'

'I been through it, few years back, when a bunch of bank robbers tried to get away.'

'*Tried?* They didn't make it?'

'Hell, no. Three died of thirst: fools filled their canteens with whiskey; died happy, mebbe. The other two were afoot because their broncs snapped legs on the flint and pumice. Not much water in there, either.' His words began to trail off and he snapped his head around, studying the country again. He swore, made no attempt to smother the epithet as he turned his gaze back to Allard. 'A herd of cows would never make it, that what you're sayin'?'

Allard nodded and the girl gasped, looked at the men swiftly. 'We-we've been following the wrong trail?'

'Been no real sign since that sandstorm swept away all tracks. We just kept riding south, in the general direction of Magdalena,' Mack said. 'I knew there was a shortcut through that country and Jones would likely remember it. It's OK for properly equipped riders; they could make a fast crossing, 'but driving a bunch of cows. . . .'

Jim shook his head. 'Can't see it.'

'Me neither,' admitted Pendle, dry, cracked lips tight and moody. 'You're right. We been loco fools! No tellin' where they turned off – or when!'

Jim didn't bother pointing out Pendle was the one in the hurry and had insisted they follow: but he knew that wasn't fair. He should have thought about that killer country earlier.

'Let's try to figure it out. We know it had to be after the sandstorm because we were finding tracks till then. We need to go back to where we know Jones was ahead of us with the herd.'

'Go back! Hell, man, we'll lose more goddamn time!'

'What's the choice? Run around chasing your tail and hope you fly off at a tangent in the right direction? You do what you want, Pendle, this is Ella's decision.'

'It damn well ain't! I'm the law and I've ordered you to help me and, by Godfrey, that's what you're gonna do!'

His hand reached his gun butt but froze when he stared into the steady, menacing muzzle of Allard's Colt. Ella drew in a sharp breath and Mack Pendle swallowed before frowning and slowly taking his hand away from the walnut pistol butt.

'By God! No wonder Jubal Clay never stood a chance agin you, Allard!'

115

Ella looked sharply at Jim and he said, 'It wasn't that way. Makes no nevermind here. Look, Pendle, we need to co-operate. We all want to catch up with Jones. We've each got some stores that have to be shared out at every stop we make – no use one of us slanting-off. You might have the coffee, but Ella has the biggest canteen with most of our water and I've got what's left of the grub. To even eat a proper meal we have to stay together – and share.'

Mack Pendle didn't have the temperament for accepting gracefully, but he nodded curtly. 'How far back you reckon?'

'We last saw definite sign of the herd this side of Temora Pass.'

'Almost a full day's ride!'

Jim merely stared and let Pendle finally simmer down. The marshal wrenched his weary, froth-caked horse's head around angrily and started riding away at an angle, northeast.

It was the right direction and Allard and the girl followed.

'I'm beginning to wonder if I'll ever see any part of that herd again, Jim.'

'We'll find it – and get it back.'

He hoped he sounded convincing because he had plenty of doubts himself.

It was well into afternoon before they found the place where they figured Jones and the herd must have turned south or south-west. Jim and Mack searched hard for tracks in the loose, wind-blown sand and when the sun dropped lower in the west,

116

both stretched out on their bellies and moved cautiously around, looking for shadows cast by the slanting sun's rays. Both found clutches of tiny mounds where the hoofs had disturbed the sand and, widening the search, were convinced this was the place.

'Can you tell if the herd is still intact?' Ella asked.

Allard knew she was thinking of Pendle saying that one of his mysterious contacts had told him Jones might keep out the Hereford bull, and the Brahmans, and hold d'Angelo to ransom.

'Can't tell, Ella,' Jim said quietly.

'There used to be a waterhole about ten miles due south.' Mack Pendle stood on a rock, shading his eyes. 'Dunno if it's still there but we could make camp and come morning we'd be bound to find their tracks in the early light.'

'If they used the waterhole.'

' 'Course they would! Every damn trail herd that comes this way uses it – or did – because the next is to hell-an'-gone in the foothills of the sierras.'

'That's men who care about the condition of their cattle,' Jim pointed out, 'looking to get the best market price . . . On paper, Jones has already sold the herd to d'Angelo. From what I know of him, he ain't the kind to worry about running a little fat off the cows – and bulls.'

Ella's mouth tightened. 'I wish I could say you're wrong, Jim, but it's exactly the kind of thing Jones would do.'

'Well, we'll see,' Pendle said, mounting stiffly.

'Be dark before we get there.'

'So? There'll be stars – *I* can find my way.'

So could Jim but he thought it was pushing too hard after the long ride in furnace heat this day. But Ella's impatience made her agree with Pendle.

So they started to ride due south.

When they broke camp early, there was no certain-sure sign that Jones and the herd had been at the scummy waterhole: although Jim found a squashed lizard in the bottom of a hoofprint that looked no more than a couple of days old. It was possible they had been here.

There was no choice now but to ride in the direction of the d'Angelo rancho. They were pushing their mounts hard but at least the animals had had their fill of water last night and there had been a patch of grass around the pool for them to graze on.

Jim was anxious to catch up with the herd before some of d'Angelo's *vaqueros* rode out to meet it. There was bound to be trouble and the Mexican *ranchero* would be within his rights to dispute Ella's ownership. Some of these old *hidalgos* were willing – and able – to stand up for their rights, even if it meant killing a bunch of *gringos*. And they could get away with it.

Jim had no wish for a fight with rawhide-tough *vaqueros* when they out-numbered him three or four to one.

But they hadn't been travelling for more than three hours when Ella called urgently, trailing the men on her slow paint.

'Jim! Mack!'

They reined down and were drawing their guns even as they turned their mounts. She was standing in the stirrups, pointing excitedly to their right – almost north.

There was a dust cloud lifting over the heatwaves quivering across the flats, barely visible against the looming greyness of a line of parched hills.

'Could that be the herd!'

Jim shook his head. 'Not in that direction, Ella.'

Mack Pendle, studying it, reached for his field-glasses in his saddle-bag but also shook his head before he brought them out. 'They ought to be further ahead than that – and the dust is too far north.'

'It *could* be the herd,' she insisted. 'You weren't certain about those tracks at the turn-off or the waterhole. They might not have swung south-west until well past the place where you thought there were tracks – or even earlier, but back along the trail we assumed they were travelling. They could have been driving more slowly than we judged.'

It was possible, but not likely.

Then Mack Pendle, looking through the field-glasses now, said tightly, 'There's a bunch liftin' that dust, all right, but a bunch of riders, comin' hell-for-leather. About seven or eight I reckon, and I can see the sun flashin' from their guns!'

He lowered the glasses and looked soberly at Allard.

'We got trouble – comin' up fast!'

The nearest cover – some low lines of sun-cracked, jagged rock faultlines – were the best part of a mile and a half away.

'*Run!*'

Jim yelled and whipped off his hat, slapping it across the rump of the slow-coach paint. It whinnied in fright or indignation or both, rear legs momentarily buckling, scrabbling wildly at the loose sand for a few seconds before finding a grip.

Ella rocked in the saddle with the jerk of the paint's lunge and Jim leaned out and slapped the animal again. It would be enough and he jammed the hat back on, holding the bay back more or less level with the paint, chaperoning the girl.

Mack Pendle was out in front, rifle in hand, riding like the wind for the line of rocks.

Jim's eyes watered with the burn of the hot wind as he turned his head to the side, watching that dust cloud.

He felt himself tighten and give an involuntary jerk as he saw how much closer it was already. He could even see the moving black line beneath it as the riders making the dust spurred in to cut them off.

It was going to be a damn close-run thing.

Damn close!

Jim Allard didn't know it at the time, but the leader of the bunch of killers he had hired in Santa Mercado – Sheriff Jake Bartells – was thinking the same thing.

'Ride like hell, you sons of bitches!' he yelled into the hot wind. 'First man to bring one of 'em down gets a bonus!'

CHAPTER 11

BLOOD AND SAND

Mack Pendle drew ahead, spurring and lashing his racing, hard-working mount. Allard, staying close to shepherd the girl in, tightened his lips. *How the hell did Pendle ever get to be a US marshal? From what he knew about the service, they didn't recruit cowards.*

Moments later, dropping back and closer, reaching out for the bridle of Ella's straining mount, Jim felt like eating his words.

A rifle began shooting from the closest entrance to the canyons. He saw the spurt of powdersmoke, but not the shooter – except for a small patch of checked shirt like Pendle was wearing. He was trying to give Allard and Ella covering fire but the pursuers were still out of range: just.

Jim saw the spurts of dust as the bullets dropped several yards in front of the closing killers. Some of them had been shooting off their guns in their enthusiasm, but the fugitives were out of range,

121

which meant Pendle was well and truly beyond the reach of their bullets.

Ella's mount was struggling and holding Jim back. She called to him to ride on, but he ignored her, kept battling with the tiring pack horse. Bullets were zipping about them now; he didn't like to think how much closer those killers must be for that to happen and was damned if he would look. Even a second's distraction could result in a mighty serious crash for them both: already the staggering bay was veering off, having brushed the sweating paint.

He glanced at the place where he had seen Mack's gunsmoke, heard the crack of the rifle, but the smoke cloud was now a few feet higher up the shale ridge above the narrow cutting that led to the canyons beyond.

The marshal had shifted to a better position: once Jim and the girl were through, he could control that narrow cutting for as long as his ammunition held out.

As Allard and the girl raced through the cutting, Jim dropping behind because of the narrow, dangerous walls, Mack Pendle got his first victim. Jim was at a slight angle to the entrance, glanced up in time to see one of the riders out in front, suddenly spill from the saddle, tumbling loosely in the dust. They were still pretty well bunched up and those behind, although they tried to rein aside, rode over the downed man. It caused chaos, horses colliding, rearing, whinnying, another rider falling, two more almost unhorsed clinging awkwardly as they fought their pitching mounts.

The girl was bringing the paint to a skidding halt: it was so weary its legs almost crossed, buckling. She dismounted awkwardly, nearly falling, clinging to the saddlehorn to help her stay on her feet.

Allard skidded his bay, wrenching hard enough on the reins to twist the horse's head around almost against his left leg. He released the reins, snatching his rifle from the saddle scabbard, freeing his boots from the stirrups and dismounting by leaping back over the bay's rump.

'Get under cover!' he snapped to the girl and ran for the position he had picked out for himself on the ride in through the cutting.

It meant climbing part way up the steep side to where a large rock jutted. He could use it for cover as long as he could find a foothold behind it. Climbing was awkward with the rifle, and he rammed it through his bullet belt, pushing it around towards his back. Using both hands now, fingers straining for a grip, some of the earth and shale crumbling under his weight, he gradually made his way up. Mack's rifle was still firing and he could hear the riders outside answering, but judging by the sounds, the marshal was keeping them away from the entrance.

Then he was behind the boulder, panting, sweat stinging his eyes, legs shaking as he searched for toeholds with his scuffed boots. There was a small uneven ledge – a ribbon-like vein of some conglomerate, not yet quite compacted enough to be called rock, but it bore his weight. He awkwardly worked the rifle free of the belt, balancing precariously. Once he thought he was falling and almost dropped the rifle in a frantic grab for a more secure hold. He eased himself in uncomfortably, back pressed against the wall where stones protruded and ground into his spine.

Then he levered a shell into the Winchester's breech, eased half his upper body out to the right and looked past the boulder.

There were eight men out there, all armed, all shooting, all intent on killing their quarry. Mack Pendle's rifle fire had driven them back twenty yards and they were now lined up in a long, shallow ditch. There was not enough cover for their mounts and Mack brought down two, winged a third.

When one of the men ran out to grab the reins of a horse getting ready to run, Jim threw his rifle to his shoulder and triggered. The man went down on the run, somersaulting and skidding. He tried to get up, groggily, and Mack put him down for keeps.

Then another rifle began firing and Jim was surprised to see Ella crouching behind an outcrop, her carbine working, bullets kicking dirt and gravel along the edge of the trench. The killers made sure they kept their heads down.

Allard grinned: those rannies out there would find they had a real fight on their hands now. No quick ride-in-and-kill here. They were going to lose some men before they could get even halfway to the cutting.

If they tried to ride out and look for another way in, they would be shot down before they could settle in the saddle.

'You see who it is?' Mack called, and Jim said no,

he hadn't yet seen anyone he knew. 'Then open your goddamn eyes! That's Jake Bartells leadin' that bunch, so don't expect no mercy.'

'I don't – and don't aim to give any. You OK, Ella?'

'Yes, Jim.' She answered readily enough but he could hear the worry edging her words. *She was game, though.*

What a trio! Jim thought: a girl rancher scared out of her wits but fighting anyway, a Federal Marshal with a bad temper and barely restrained hostility towards a drifter who had had his fill of fighting during his eventful lifetime.

They were thrown together, trying to ward off a bunch of gold-hungry killers led by a sheriff who, for all they knew, was plumb loco: there seemed to be no other motive for the attack.

But the time for rationalizing was past: that same loco sheriff had organized his men into firing all together and the line of rifles blasted the cutting and the rocks above, seeking each of their hiding places. Allard ducked as two slugs whined off the boulder in front of him, a little dust spurting. He glimpsed the girl throwing herself down, arms covering her head. Mack Pendle flattened back against his sheltering rock as lead spattered against it.

A pause – very short – then the rattling clash of rifle levers carrying faintly to the defenders. As they lifted their own weapons to retaliate, the guns in the hollow below blasted once more in a volley that was only a little ragged and off-time. Jim and the others ducked, almost caught by the raking hail of bullets.

Allard hunkered against his boulder and stayed

put this time. Within seconds another volley tore across the guarded entrance to the canyons.

'Must have plenty of ammo!' called Mack Pendle, not sounding worried at all.

'That, or someone's making a dash for it while we've got our heads down.'

After a brief silence – and yet another volley that made them stay hidden so they could not see what was happening below – the marshal snarled, 'You could be right!'

'Want to take a look?'

'Why don't you? You're highest.'

'I've already looked through a crack in the rock in front of me,' called Ella breathlessly. 'I think two men rode out of the hollow – the hoofbeats were covered by the rifle volleys.'

Allard heard Pendle swearing, but asked the girl, 'Which way?'

She had to wait until the next volley had raked their shelters and the echoes died away.

'To our left. But I think one kept riding on along the ridge face.'

'Gonna come in from two directions,' opined Mack, at last getting his rifle working and smoking, emptying a full magazine along the edge of the trench that hid the remaining attackers.

'*We* don't have a helluva lot of ammo!' Jim cautioned.

Mack didn't reply, but his rifle fell silent.

Jim waited but there was no volley from below this time: maybe they didn't have as much ammunition as he had first thought. Or, maybe they had simply gained their objective: gotten two riders away while making the defenders stay low.

He hitched around awkwardly – and carefully – his boots slipping off the narrow ledge. He gritted his teeth as sharp rock edges raked his shin and lower leg.

But he could see up to the rim of the cutting from here, ran his gaze back and forth, looking for a crumpled hat or glinting gun barrel breaking the skyline up there.

Nothing!

Now he began to get worried. What in the hell kind of trick were they trying to pull? They had managed to get two riders out and he expected them to close in on the area where they were hiding, one from each side. But there was nothing breaking the silhouette of the notched rim for as far as he could see in either direction.

There had been plenty of time for the men to climb into position from the other side of the ridge. . . .

No! Not from the other side: from *this* side, right below them, while they had their attention on the high wall.

He almost fell as he spun around, hung on by one hand, rifle swinging in the other, and looked down between his boot toes. There was a moving shadow – moving up under Mack Pendle's position. In fact, the man had slithered down from the place he had climbed to on his belly and was now easing through between the legs of Pendle's restless mount.

The marshal could not see him from where he

crouched. The man suddenly reared up, six-gun raised.

'Mack!' Jim yelled and fired his rifle. At the same time two rifles fired from the hollow and one bullet whined off his boulder, stinging his face with rock dust. He reeled back and another gun barked from above and lead seared across and down his left arm. He lost his grip and fell, rolling and bouncing off rock, crashing into the wall and losing his rifle. His legs took the jar as he landed and then collapsed under him. He hit his head and blood flowed as he crouched there, dazed.

Then a voice called from the rim: 'Hold it right there, Pendle! I've got the girl covered. You throw down your gun or I shoot her.'

'Makes no nevermind to me,' Pendle called back, but he was staring into the sun now that outlined the rim and could barely make out the man who was making the threat.

The man on the rim laughed. 'OK! Lady, you're outa luck. No nevermind to Pendle, even less to me!'

The rifle cracked, but a second before it did Jim Allard's Colt roared and the man up there lifted to his toes, shuddered, and followed his tumbling rifle down to crash onto the rocks.

'*My God*!' cried Ella, hand holding her head.

Mack Pendle was more descriptive in his exclamation as he looked down from his position only a few feet above where Jim crouched, smoking gun in hand.

'How long you ride with Jubal Clay?' he grated, after running out of epithets.

'Not long. Why?' Allard was curious at the question.

'Long enough to teach you how to draw and shoot? Christ Almighty, I've seen gunslingers from Montana to Mexico and I never seen none faster than the way you drew and fired just then – and that includes Jubal Clay!'

'Pure exaggeration.' Jim reloaded quickly, reached for his rifle with his left arm which was bleeding freely now.

'You're hurt!' Ella cried from her position, concerned.

'Bullet gouged me is all – never mind that. We still got four or five of them varmints out there trying to nail us and it's not long till sundown.'

He gestured to the sun disappearing over the edge of the rim now.

'They'll use the darkness!' Pendle said grimly.

'So can we,' Allard said softly, awkwardly knotting his neckerchief around his bleeding arm. It was beginning to hurt now and would stiffen with the chill of the desert night.

But that was the least of their worries.

They were separated from their horses and if those snakes out there knew their business – and they had demonstrated that they did – the mounts would be watched. As soon as they showed up to try and recover them, the night would be torn apart by rifle fire.

Thirst had been with them most of the day and it came again with the darkness. Their canteens were on their saddles and their saddles were on the mounts – which were under the guns of Bartells and his killers.

Five of them left. Plenty to split up, three, maybe only two, to watch their horses, the others. . . .

Jim tensed as there was a brief rattle of stones falling. Did a careless boot dislodge some gravel caught between rocks or was it just a natural fall as the rocks cooled with the onset of night?

This was not the time to make the wrong choice.

His rifle was fully loaded, as was his Colt. He had no spurs to worry about, jingling or scraping, to give him away. Mack Pendle was quiet and he wasn't even sure if the marshal was in his position. The night was black as a stovepipe, the stars only now beginning to appear, a sprinkle at a time. The girl? He didn't dare call out, but he thought she was still in position, or had maybe moved into a crevice he had noticed close by. He had tried to urge her to do so by signs before darkness closed in but wasn't sure she had understood. She would be safer there, but wherever she was right now, he wasn't sure: he just had to hope she was all right.

Because he was on the move.

Already, thinking about Ella, he was leaving his precarious perch, rifle pushed through his bullet belt at the back again, leaving both hands free. His fingers were numb in no time, groping and sliding across the rough surface, taking the strain of his body while his boots sought a hold. Leather scraped once or twice and he froze, hanging, literally, by his fingertips. The blood pounding in his ears prevented him from hearing any small sounds: for all he knew, the two men who had ridden out of the hollow could be within feet of him, just waiting for his head to appear over a ledge, cocked guns at the ready.

No! That was no way to think: danger and disaster lay in that direction. His boots found a hold at last and aching leg muscles lifted him up another foot. He rested, turning his head left and right slowly. To the right he could discern the outline of the edge of the rim against a pale nest of stars, but to the left there was only a void.

He tensed, starting to the right, but some instinct made him change his mind and move left, into the unknown. Hand feeling inch by inch, boots moving over even less distance each time, he made his way along an unseen ledge that couldn't have been more than two or three inches wide. Breath came hard and ragged and he kept his mouth open, trying to quieten the gasps. Resting, arms, legs, entire body quivering with strain, he swung his head awkwardly to the right. His wounded arm ached and was bleeding freely again.

He froze: the edge of the rim was still vaguely outlined against the stars and, as he looked, he saw a man's head and shoulders break the line. There was no way he could tell if the man was looking in this direction, but he tightened his grip with his left fingers – they felt like they were about to break – and dropped his right hand towards his gun butt. The movement upset his balance and his body swung halfway out from the rockface, boots scraping as he fought to stay on the ledge. All strain was on his left arm.

There was no mistake now: the man on the rim had heard him, bringing his rifle over and up to his shoulder. Allard's Colt came up blazing, two shots. He heard one snarl away in ricochet from the rim edge and then a grunt and the clatter of a falling rifle. The man slumped, upper body hanging over the edge, arms dangling loosely.

Now the other man would know exactly where Jim was!

He hung there, knowing Ella and Mack would be wondering if he was the one who had been shot. But he couldn't hold the position for long, all his weight on his left fingers and boot toes. He was just holstering his gun when a voice almost directly above called quietly,

'Hal? Who you shootin' at? *Hal!*'

He must have spotted his pard's body and Jim heard the low curse, the movements of a man readying his guns.

Looking up, Allard saw the man's shape outlined against the star glow as he brought his gun over the rim and started shooting wildly down the rockface. He was a yard or two over to Jim's right but would work his fire back this way. There was only one thing to do.

Allard's Colt blazed and the man up there yelled, rolled back from the edge. Jim holstered the gun now and took his chances by starting straight up. His heart was thundering as he groped for and used precarious holds that a cat would have passed up. Head dizzy with exertion, lungs feeling ready to explode, he gave one final heave and was over the rim, rolling away from the edge, gun in hand again.

The wounded man was sobbing in pain, saw Allard's sprawled body and tried to reach his rifle. Jim rolled closer, gasping, his own rifle digging into his back.

The man slumped, hit badly. In the faint light, Jim saw it was a total stranger. Wetness gleamed on the man's chest as he lay on his side, watching with wide eyes, patiently waiting for Jim to kill him.

'Where you from?'

After some heavy gasping and bubbling cough, the man slurred something that only later Allard deciphered as 'Santa Mercado'.

'Bartells paying you?' A weary nod. 'Why's he want to kill us?'

'Dun-no. Wants . . . woman . . . alive . . .'

That stopped Jim for a moment. 'Why?'

The man shook his head and it was too much of an effort. His head fell forward and although he breathed a little longer there was no more response from him.

CHAPTER 12

SPANISH DON

'Bartells!'

Jim's voice echoed and boomed around the canyons as he called down from the rim.

'You there, Jake?'

No answer.

'Well, I *know* you are so just listen . . . I've nailed both the men you sent after us. You're only three now, and so are we, but we have the high ground and we can pin you down till daylight. After that – it's anybody's guess what might happen.'

'I damn well knew soon's I saw you, you were gonna be a pain in my ass!'

'I can be a pain to everybody, Jake. I dunno what your cards are in this deal and don't care. You want to make a run for it during the night, go ahead. If you're still there come sun-up, pick yourself a good spot for your grave.'

Allard flattened himself, expecting the angry sheriff to take a potshot but nothing happened. He lay there, listening. Ella and Mack Pendle had the good sense to remain silent so Bartells and his cronies didn't get a fix on their positions.

He hoped Bartells would pull out: he was low on ammunition and knew the others must be, too. That was one of the reasons he didn't want it to come to a shootout at dawn. Another was thirst: they needed to get to the water in their saddle canteens.

That thought gave him an idea. Crouching low, trying to forget the pain in his still bleeding arm, he scouted around and eventually found where the two men he had killed had ground-hitched their mounts.

There were large saddle canteens, two on each horse. One was less than half-full, one just over half, and two almost filled right up. He left the ground-hitching in place, slung the canteens awkwardly, holding his rifle with his free hand, and then had the problem of finding a way down.

Before he was successful he heard the sudden rapid tattoo of hoofs from below. Crouching on the edge he strained to see and could just make out the dark shapes coming out of the far end of the trench. One – two – *damn!* Where was the third man? Then suddenly he appeared and Jim had the impression the man was wounded, awkward in the saddle.

He kept his word: he could have picked them off with a little luck and a magazine full of bullets but he let them go, the hoofbeats fading gradually.

They would still have to be on the alert in case Bartells circled back, but for now, he would have time to find an easy way down and share out the water with the others.

For the first time in two days they would be able to drink their fill – and know there was still more than enough left for a few more days.

If they hadn't located Jones and the herd by then, they were never going to do it.

Wendell Jones was slightly daunted when he saw the size of the d'Angelo rancho. It wasn't the first time he had seen it, but he had forgotten how large it was.

The house was white adobe, sprawled over the slope of a rise, giving a view over the long bend of the river. Clumps of trees grew here and there, either naturally or had been planted by d'Angelo's ancestors. Through the arched gateway, he glimpsed more greenery around the house, the splash of colour in the flower gardens, and a long cool gallery.

The two *vaqueros* who had escorted him in took him into the walled area and motioned for him to wait in the shade of a sycamore. A barefoot peon ran up and took his horse away to groom and grain.

'Not too much water,' Jones called, standing confidently, aware of his grime and dishevelled appearance but uncaring.

A servant brought a tray with a clay jug beaded with condensation and before the man had placed it on the small wrought-iron table, Jones snatched it and drank directly from the jug. It was some kind of citrus drink, and against his parched, raw throat it was nectar of the gods.

The servant went and two men appeared at the

end of the gallery. He knew the short, fat one was d'Angelo. The lean man in full *vaquero* get-up, with two six-guns in an ornate *buscadero* rig, would be Rey Lando, a bodyguard with a tough reputation along the Border. A killer, and lightning on the draw.

'*Bienvenido* Señor Jones – I do not see my cattle.'

Wendell Jones grinned, turned and waved his hat towards the line of blue-hazed hills. 'On their way, *señor*. My men have had a difficult drive.'

The *ranchero* strolled across, closely followed by the hawk-faced Lando, and sat down in a chair opposite Jones. His dark eyes were sharp and probing.

'You do not, of course, wish me to pay extra because of your . . . difficulties.'

Jones forced a laugh. *This old ranchero was mighty sharp.* Resigned now, he dropped the idea, and said, 'Of course not, *señor*. That is my responsibility – though it will eat into my small profit.'

'The way of the cattle business – I have been expecting you for several days.'

'Difficulties, as I said. *Bandidos and* a stampede.'

D'Angelo straightened. 'The bulls?'

Jones lifted a hand. 'All OK. We cut them out early to save them.' His gaze shifted a little despite an effort to keep it squarely on the Mexican's face. 'Fact is, I kept them separate to the herd – not easy. Not with all them cows and comely young heifers makin' eyes at 'em.'

'I am not partial to innuendo, *señor*. I have a sense of humour, but not when I am doing business or in the company of women.'

There were no women about that Jones could see,

except one hanging clothes on a line at a rear corner of the *hacienda*. But he took the hint and would watch his mouth now.

'Your pardon, Señor d'Angelo.'

The Mexican made no acknowledgement, asked, 'When may I expect to see my herd?'

'Well, it ain't exactly your herd yet, *señor*, you know what I mean.'

'*Sí*, I know exactly what you mean. You will have your payment, in gold, as you requested. But, when will I see the herd?'

'In an hour or two. See? There's a smudge of dust already against the foothills? We could settle-up while they're comin' in.'

D'Angelo turned to Rey Lando. 'Send some *vaqueros* to help.' As the silent bodyguard strode away towards the stables and corrals area, the Mexican gave Jones his attention again. 'Your price is high. I expect the herd to live up to my expectations.'

'They will. Just allow for the hard drive here and you'll see you've got a fine bargain. Few days rest in one of them good pastures yonder and they'll be better'n anythin' you've got in this neck of the woods.'

'We will see. How long have they been in the breeding programme?'

Jones's face straightened a little, but he was a quick thinker. 'Dunno all that much about 'em – Mr Norton just hired me and my outfit to drive 'em down to you.'

D'Angelo frowned, his moon face seeming to tighten. 'Then you are a trail-driver, and not a breeder?'

'That's right. That breedin' stuff's way beyond me.'

'It is hoped you have exercised due care on the long drive! These are not ordinary cattle.'

'I know that, *señor*. I followed Mr Norton's instructions to the letter. Losses were few – a couple on the narrow trail over the lava ridges and one in the canyons.'

D'Angelo frowned, fidgeted, looked up sharply as Lando returned and told him in a quiet voice that men had been sent out to meet the herd. The lean man pointed and the *ranchero* seemed calmer when he saw four riders already leaving by the gateway. He took out a cigarillo and Rey Lando leaned forward, snapping a vesta into flame on a thumbnail, holding it for his boss.

'I could use one of them,' Jones said. 'Ain't had any tobacco for a couple of days.'

D'Angelo puffed smoke. He gave no indication he had heard Jones and the *Americano* flushed, jaw thrusting a little, muscles along it tightened.

'OK,' he breathed. He picked up the clay jug and drank from it again, eyes slanting towards the *ranchero*, pleased to see the man's expression of disapproval. He wiped his mouth on the torn, filthy sleeve of his shirt, set the jug down hard enough to slop some of the contents on to the table – on d'Angelo's side. The Mexican had to move his chair slightly as the small stream trickled over the table edge.

'Have care, *gringo*!' Rey Lando's voice was cold, warning, barely raised above a whisper.

139

'Oh, hell yeah, I'm noted for havin' care, *amigo*, 'specially for my own hide.'

Lando remained expressionless, but his eyes never left Jones as the man stood, stretched the kinks out of his body after days of hard riding, wandered over to a small wall fountain, studying the moulded clay cherubs surrounding it.

The herd arrived soon after and was turned into the pastures, the *vaqueros* reporting in rapid Spanish. D'Angelo snapped up his head, glaring at Jones.

'My men report unattended injuries! Some appear to be from falls, others from – what? Spurs? Whips?' He stood up angrily as Jones shrugged. 'You are so stupid that you use normal trail driving methods on such a special herd?'

'Look, *señor*, we brought 'em across a corner of hell. We had bandits on the skyline watchin' every move, water was short, sandstorms. My job was to get 'em here as quick as I could. None of them injuries are serious. Hell, some I've seen at trail's end would make you lose your supper. . . .'

He let his words fade, aware of the Mexican's simmering anger.

'Mr Norton will not be pleased when I drop my price. *If* I even decide to buy a damaged herd.'

Jones pulled at an earlobe. 'Well, now, Señor d'Angelo – we had a deal. Ten tousand dollars in gold.'

'For a herd in good condition.'

Jones swept an arm towards the pastures where riders were still hazing the cattle in. 'Go take a look

– but the price remains the same.'

Rey Lando looked to his boss for orders, but d'Angelo mashed out his cigarillo and strode across the yard to where a stable hand waited with saddled horse. He mounted and rode away towards the pastures. Lando remained, regarding Jones contemptuously.

'You *gringo* fool! To dare speak to the *padrone* that way.'

'Relax, *pistolero*, I ain't stupid enough to try and draw agin you. Couldn't get me somethin' stronger to drink than this stuff, could you?' He indicated the jug.

Lando sneered and turned his back on Jones. '*Gringo* pig!'

Jones's hard eyes narrowed as they waited in silence until d'Angelo returned, riding his thoroughbred Arab in fast, skidding to a halt, face flushed with anger.

'Where are the breeding bulls?' he demanded. 'The cows and heifers and even the calves have obviously been mistreated – but that can be put right. But . . . where . . . are . . . my bulls?'

'Aw, yeah. Well, I told you we separated 'em so's they didn't get caught up in any more stampedes. I mean, I know how necessary they are to your breedin' programme – can't run it without 'em, can you? That's why it's gonna cost you *another* ten thousand – in gold – to get your hands on 'em.' He held up one hand as Lando started towards him. 'Uh-uh. Anythin' happens to me, my men've got orders to shoot them goddamn pesky bulls, one by one. The

Brahmans first, and the good ol' well-hung Hereford last. Now I mean it, *pistolero* – and your boss knows it. Just look at his face!' Jones's mocking smile widened. 'Hell, he knows he don't have a choice. Ain't that right, Don d'Angelo. . . ?'

'You are a very smart – and ruthless man, Jones. It is unusual for me to be in such a position as this. You may win, or see it as winning, but I will never forget. Never!'

CHAPTER 13

FAST AS
THEY COME

They had left Bartells and his remaining men far behind – they hoped.

Riding now on the edge of the desert, coming into low ranges and more and more vegetation, Allard slowed the pace. Mack Pandle knew why but had to grouch just the same.

'Go much slower and we'll be travellin' backwards!'

'Maybe right into Bartells.'

'He won't bother followin' us. He's still hell-for-leather after Jones, so he'll be heading for Magdalena.'

'Take the chance if you want,' Jim offered but Mack didn't reply.

Ella sounded worried when she asked, 'Couldn't Bartells have got ahead of us somehow and be waiting in those hills and gulches?'

'*Could* be, but as Mack says he'll likely go flat out after Jones now.' Seeing she was still worried, Jim added, 'I'll scout ahead when we reach the foothills proper.'

'You stay where you can be seen.'

Allard ignored the marshal but Ella still seemed apprehensive.

The change in scenery was a big contrast to the last few days of riding through a wasteland. Trees and grasses began to appear, even the odd wildflower. Birds, too, screeched across the sky with a thrumming of dozens of wings. Jim watched their general direction for later reference. The big river was some way off yet, but it was clear that these hills must receive some rain. Which meant there would be waterholes. Once Jim thought he heard distant gunfire but it was too far off to be sure. He led the way up a winding trail and less than halfway to the end, they saw a churned dark patch below, widening as it reached the edge of the plain.

'That looks like sign of a stampede to me. A trail herd at normal speed wouldn't tear up the ground that way.'

Ella drew alongside and agreed. Even Pendle grunted affirmatively. Using field-glasses they found the start of the churned-up ground. It seemed dry and unlikely to be much disturbed by the passing of a trail herd, the cattle weary after a desert crossing. But when the stampede fever hit, those hoofs would have dug in hard.

'Them fainter tracks must've been made after they

144

quietened 'em down,' Pendle growled adjusting focus.

'Why the hell would they drive a herd so close to these hills from the flats? The tracks are almost in the foothills.'

Before anyone could put forth a possible explanation, all three tensed and snapped their heads around, looking up the sloping trail.

What they heard was the unmistakable bellowing of a beast in distress – a large one with a deep chest that sent the bawling cry echoing through the hills.

'That'll be the Hereford!' Ella exclaimed.

The trio spurred their mounts, drawing closer to the sound as it continued. They reached a section where they could hear it plainly but the direction seemed hard to locate. A sloping rock cliff, the face studded with boulders of all sizes, rose before them. They scouted around, looking for some sort of pass. It was the marshal who found a narrow winding passage, the entrance of which was hidden by the natural placement of two egg-shaped boulders, one slightly in front and to one side of the other, masking the opening.

They went through with drawn guns, the bellowing almost deafening now, and came out onto a ledge above a small grassy canyon that had a muddy waterhole at one end.

The Hereford was belly deep in the mud, several feet out from the bank and its wallowing struggles were sinking it further each time it tried to plunge for firmer ground.

The men looked around, rifles at the ready, while

Ella prepared the ropes. There was no sign of anyone and soon their loops were on the distressed bull and the horses were straining to ease it out enough so the suction holding it would break. The rescue attempt made the animal bellow even louder, its struggling becoming frantic – but futile.

Allard sighed and put his bay into the muddy water, reeling in his rope to keep it taut as he approached the bull. The animal's eyes rolled and followed him suspiciously. Saliva flew as it raised its head and bawled loudly. Then Jim leaned from the saddle, grabbed the mud-slippery tail, and heeled the bay forward, alongside the bull's rump. Rope around the saddlehorn, he kept the strain on the tail. It bent the thick base, grinding away at the end of the spine. It caused the bull pain and the bellowing increased. The hind end began to jerk and the animal thrashed its rear legs wildly – breaking the mud's suction with slurping sounds. One final heave and Jim laid the bull's rump over on one side and with the others shifting their ropes and using their horses, they dragged the protesting beast to firmer ground. It scrabbled wildly, tossing its head. The horses lunged away, whinnying, dodging the down-slashing horns. They flipped their ropes clear as the Hereford splashed through the muddy water and out on to the bank. It shook itself, bellowed a final protest and hip-swayed away to the nearest patch of grass, dripping mud.

Jim was a mess but found a small pool of reasonably clear water and washed up as best he could. The desert sun would not take long to dry him out.

'How did that bull get here?' Ella asked after thanking the men.

There was only one narrow entrance on the same level as the canyon floor, leading between high sandstone walls. Beyond it lay yet another canyon, longer, wider – and down below there, near a small creek, the two Brahmans stood looking towards the riders.

'No sign of the rest of the herd,' the girl said quietly.

Allard spoke slowly. 'Seems to me, Jones may've cut out the seed bulls and hidden 'em away in here.' Ella looked at him swiftly. 'Could be holding d'Angelo to ransom – isn't that what your contact told you, Mack?'

Pendle nodded. 'Somethin' like that . . .'

'Someone's coming!' Ella said suddenly, pointing to a small dust cloud past the far end of the long canyon below.

'Maybe Jones—'

Mack Pendle bared his teeth, checking his rifle.

'Let's give 'em a welcome – whoever the hell they are!'

'Well, why don't we leave the "welcome" 'til later while we have us a leetle talk?'

They whirled and stared at two men standing on a small ledge several feet above their heads. One was Jake Bartells, the other most likely one of the men who had traded lead with the trio some days earlier.

Their rifles covered the girl and the two men.

Bartells gestured to the muddy Hereford. 'Saved us some trouble, I see. We seen camp-fire smoke comin' from in these hills earlier. Kerry here knows the general area. Found us a couple of Jones's men, left to guard the bulls, I reckon. Two of his best hard-cases: put up a helluva fight. Got Kerry's brother, Slim, but we nailed 'em. Then we heard that bull bellowin' fit to cave in the damn sky. Been lookin' for a way in here – and now we found it.'

'The bulls are mine, Jake!' Ella said sharply. 'Jones tricked me, but I've paid money for them.'

Bartells scowled. 'Jones is mighty good at trickin' folk! Told me only a few thousand was involved and my share was one thousand!' He almost spat he was so mad. 'Then, havin' a drink with Banker Morgan and he lets slip he loaned you *ten thousand* and you arranged with the Bisbee bank to pay it in cash. An' now he's tryin' to make more with the damn bulls!'

Bartells was angry, almost choking on his words, and Allard knew the man must be involved in the crooked deal: felt he was missing out on his rightful share.

'How come you're nosing in at all, Bartells?' asked Allard and the sheriff shuttled his hard gaze to him.

He stared a long minute and then looked at Ella. 'Well, Jones and me sort of come to an arrangement a long time ago. I kept him up-to-date on Ella's affairs and he used the info to work out a way to pay her back for puttin' him away in Yuma.'

Ella was white-faced but she nodded gently, look-ing at Jim. 'That's typical Jones. But I thought you and I were on reasonably friendly terms, Jake?'

His mouth twisted with bitterness. 'That's what you thought, huh? Well, you wasn't too friendly after you got your divorce – recollect?'

Her mouth opened and she stared in genuine surprise. 'Why – that time at the hoedown for Bridie and Solomon Waite's fiftieth wedding anniversary? You – you were drunk, and lonely! I never took you seriously – what you proposed.' Her face reddened a little at the memory. 'And I never held it against you.'

'You made me look a damn fool!' Bartells grated. 'In front of all them folk! You gimme a peck on the cheek, patted my head, for Chris'sake! Then blew me a kiss and told me to go home and sleep it off!' He was trembling now. 'I was the town *lawman*, and you treated me like I was some damn fresh kid! Well, I never forgot it!'

'You're miserable, Jake,' Allard told him flatly. 'A grown man, can't take a "no thanks" in good spirit, has to nurse it like a surly brat and turn on a decent woman who treated you a damn sight better than you deserved.'

'Jim, it's all right—'

'No it ain't all right!' Bartells snapped, nostrils flaring. 'I've seen townsfolk laughing behind their hands when I pass, pokin' fun at me! Never game to say anythin' out loud—'

'Maybe because there was nothing to say, Jake,' Jim pointed out. 'Maybe you imagined the lot.'

'I never imagined what she done to me at that hoedown! An' I was happy Jones had found a way to get back at her, happy enough to help him – 'cept he double-crossed me, and no one does that and gets away with it.'

Allard shook his head in disgust and then Mack Pendle, taking advantage of Bartells' distraction and using Jim's body as a cover, drew his six-gun and spurred his mount forward at the same time, shooting fast.

Jake Bartells hadn't held the sheriff's job all these years because he was soft or slow. He dropped to one knee even as the man beside him staggered, struck by Mack's lead. Going down, the man triggered his rifle and Pendle's mount lurched, fell as the marshal tumbled from the saddle.

Bartells' smoking rifle muzzle was swinging towards Allard when Jim palmed up his Colt, the bay nervously jumping. Jim's first shot missed but the second caught Bartells as he lunged to one side, hammering him down. He sprawled and fell off the ledge, landing hard at the bottom.

Jim leapt from the saddle, tossing his reins to the girl, and ran to kneel by Bartells. The lawman was dead, neck broken, so he moved to the other man who lay a few feet away. But he died before he could answer Allard's first question.

'Them riders must've have heard the shootin',' Mack called. 'They're spreadin' out – I make it five or six. Couple went to ground, but could be another one or two . . .'

He was right: the riders had spread out but they were still making their way towards the foothills, the sun glinting off drawn guns now. Allard ran the glasses over the men. He knew d'Angelo by sight and also Rey Lando – had seen the man in action in a Gulf port a couple of years back. Lightning-fast and murderous. Jones he recognized, but the other two were just nondescript *gringos*, who were probably

Jones's sidekicks.

'I make it five.' He handed the glasses to the girl who swept them over the riders swiftly.

Her mouth tightened. 'Surely Jones hasn't already made his deal with d'Angelo!'

'I'd say it's well underway. Can't make out their faces in much detail but just look at the way the Mexican's riding – not Lando, d'Angelo – see how stiff he is? And if it shows at this distance, the way he's built, I reckon he's holding down a volcano – and pretty damn soon he's gonna erupt.'

'He's not the only one!' Ella said sharply. 'These are my bulls and he's not going to take them from me! And I want my herd that I've paid for, too!'

'We'll have to settle it through gunsmoke,' the marshal said quietly, watching the riders drawing closer, starting up the rise of the foothills now. He moved his grip on his rifle, thumb hovering over the hammer spur. 'Those rannies don't look like they're here to palaver.'

'They don't even know what's happened yet,' the girl said.

'They heard the shooting, Ella, that's all they need. They'll know something's wrong.'

'Damn! They just rode through the cuttin' and are outa sight behind that spine of rock!' Pendle was agitated.

'Wait.'

They didn't have long. Jim had hardly spoken the word when Jones's voice called: 'Larry? Frenchy?'

'Shovellin' coal for Old Nick, Jones!' called Pendle, laughing harshly. 'You want to go see 'em?

Just step out a moment and say "howdy"!'

A brief silence. 'Who the hell's that?'

'US Marshal Mack Pendle, Jones. End of the trail for you.'

'I dunno you, Pendle, but you seem to have a good imagination.'

'Fact, you scum! Senator Parrish wants the man who raped and killed his wife and daughter – don't care how. Orders are just bring you in: dead or alive. You like your choices?'

A bullet whined off the rockface above their heads and all three ducked instinctively.

'I see you've made your choice, Jones! Fine with me!'

Mack rose and raked the spine of rock with five shots, chips and dust flying, the lead snarling like maddened hornets.

'You're wasting ammo,' Jim told the marshal.

Mack was breathing faster than normal now that he was this close to his quarry. He threw Allard a cold look and thumbed home fresh cartridges through the rifle's loading gate.

'What about d'Angelo?' Ella asked quietly.

Jim nodded, raised his voice. 'Señor d'Angelo! You there?'

'Sí! Who am I speaking to?'

'Jim Allard. You come for the bulls?'

'That was the plan.' The Mexican could not keep the edge of bitterness from his voice. 'I am to pay ten thousand in gold for them – I have already paid a like amount for the herd!'

'He's robbing you, señor!' Ella called suddenly. 'I

152

already paid him ten thousand for the herd, including the bulls. He posed as Beaumont Norton and got the money through the Bisbee bank. Then he stole the herd and drove it down to your *rancho* and apparently sold them again – and is now holding you to ransom for the seed bulls.'

'*Sí*, Señora Jones – that is what has happened. You must think me a fool for allowing it.'

'Not with Jones behind the deal!'

'Gee! Thanks, Ella! That's the first compliment you've paid me in a coon's age.' Wendell Jones chuckled.

'And the last, Wendell! You're even a worse snake than I knew!'

'Ah, well, you learn a lot of things – in Yuma!'

'You've never forgiven me for that, have you?'

'No – and never intend to. Not even when I've ruined you and you're grovellin' at my feet for mercy.'

'That's something you'll never see!'

While Ella was exchanging these pleasantries with Jones, Mack Pendle and Allard slipped away to the side, crouching behind some bigger boulders. The marshal signed that he would go downslope on his side and approach the spine of rock that way. Jim nodded and started down the other side.

The girl and Jones were still arguing and insulting each other, but Allard wasn't listening to the words, only the sound of the voices. *Keep him going, Ella, hold his attention.*

But what about d'Angelo? What would the fat Mexican be doing? Listening to Jones and Ella rehashing their marital problems would hold no interest for him – what would he do? Sit and wait, chewing his nails? And what about Rey Lando? That man was no fool and he took his job of looking out for Don d'Angelo's interests mighty seriously.

He wouldn't just stand there, bored, awaiting orders. He would *act!*

Jim had no sooner formed the thought than he caught a movement out of the corner of his left eye.

Lando was coming out from behind the spine, at this end, nearest where Jim crouched. He would not be visible from above and Ella was right into her stride now and probably wouldn't notice him even if he did show himself inadvertently.

The bodyguard was crouched, down on one knee, bleak gaze studying the rockface and the ledge where the girl was and, he believed hopefully, Allard and Pendle were, too.

Jim could see Lando in profile: the man was frowning. Then he started to look around suspiciously.

He knows! He hasn't heard Mack or me since Ella started in on Jones and now he's figured it out – she's holding Jones's' attention while we—

Lando saw him.

Jim had started to ease back into his cover but sun glinted from the rifle barrel as he changed hands, catching Lando's attention.

The man was already on his feet, both hands flashing to his guns. They cleared the buscadero rig at unbelievable speed, levelled and blasted instantaneously. Jim slammed backwards, dropping his rifle, one bullet spraying him with rock chips, the other clipping the brim of his hat, knocking it askew on his head. Irritably, he used his stiffening left arm to knock it away from his face and dived forward as Lando's gun fired again.

Because of Allard's forward motion, Lando shot too high, but even so one slug seared the heel of Jim's right boot, kicking his leg violently. It threw him onto his left side as he drew and fired his Colt, three fast shots and a fourth for good measure. Rey Lando reared to his toes and began to crumple, stark surprise on his hawk-like face before it settled into the blankness of death.

Mack Pendle was shooting now, his rifle filling the cutting with its echoes. Allard thought Ella was screaming something but couldn't be sure, as he leapt up, running in behind the spine of rock.

D'Angelo was sitting up in the dirt, blood trickling down his face from a fresh gash across his forehead where Jones had gunwhipped him.There was no sign of the outlaw and Jim halted, started reloading his Colt.

'Where'd he go?'

The Mexican was dazed but Jim shook him roughly and asked again. He lifted one fat arm, pointing up the slope.

Ella!

Allard started around the end of the spine and found Mack Pendle sagging amongst the rocks, blood on his shirt front, face twisted in pain.

Allard dropped to one knee beside him, pulled his hand away from the gushing chest wound.

'Hell!' he breathed, not meaning for the marshal

to hear the word.

'I-I know – it's bad. He's gone . . . after . . . Ella. Just get him, Jim, don't worry about me . . . but come back and tell . . . me you . . . you got him if I'm still . . . breathin'. . . .'

Allard squeezed the man's blood-slippery hand: he knew the marshal would be dead in a very short time. He started up the slope, taking Mack's rifle with him. He hadn't gone far before two shots crashed from above and lead whined past his face. Jim dropped in against the boulder.

'Don't bother comin' up, Allard! I've got her and all I gotta do is swing the rifle and pull the trigger. You wouldn't make one foot closer before she dies.'

'Then you'll die, Jones. You got my word on that.'

'Well, I ain't gonna say it won't matter, long as I nail her first, 'cos I still got a lotta livin' to do. And I aim to do it! *Wh-what're you doin'! Look out!*'

Jones suddenly yelled in alarm and Allard instinctively ducked as gravel pattered down the slope about his shoulders. He looked up and saw Jones's body hurtling down, sliding and bouncing, the man desperately trying to grab protruding rocks for support. He managed to break his fall a little but struck hard, along to Allard's right, the wind blasting out of him.

'Ella?'

'I-I'm all right, Jim! I – while he was boasting to you I-I pushed him. . . .' Her voice broke, shocked at her action.

'You did good, Ella.' Then Jones wavered to his feet, left arm hanging at an awkward angle but his right fist gripping his Colt. He swayed as he began firing and Jim's rifle crashed once as he dropped to one knee.

Jones shuddered, took another halting step forward and then fell off his small ledge to crash down into the cutting.

As the echoes died away, Allard heard the girl stifling a sob.

'Stay there, Ella, I'm coming to get you.'

'I can't believe it, Jim! I never thought d'Angelo would agree to sharing the bulls!'

'Well, not exactly sharing – you're charging him a stud fee, I hope.'

'It's called a "breeding" fee and yes – we've agreed on that.'

They were sitting on the porch of the Panhandle ranch house, looking out across the pastures to where Norton's – now Ella's – herd grazed. D'Angelo had agreed to the cattle resting on his pastures until the wounds sustained during Jones's rough trail drive were healed. Then Ella sent a crew down, under Jim Allard, to bring them back by the regular trail, slow-paced, following the water and grass.

D'Angelo had recovered his gold from Jones's saddle gear and, though reluctant to lose the herd, really only wanted the seed bulls to mate with his own experimental breeders. So, being a Spanish gentleman of the old school, he had allowed Ella to claim the herd on the condition that she allowed him to use her seed bulls on request, provided it was suitable. Legal papers had been laboriously drawn-up, finally, to both their satisfaction.

'You'll be able to pay off the bank, now.'

She smiled ruefully. 'Not too quickly – d'Angelo won't need the bulls very often – but I'll manage somehow.'

He knew it was worrying her and when she reached out for Jubal Clay's saddle rig which had been rubbed with neat's-foot oil and was now drying in the sun on the porch rail, he knew she wanted to change the subject.

'I'm having Bingo Reed, our carpenter, cut out a length from the last surviving plank from our original home in Kentucky. He's going to smooth it and polish it and then we'll mount the plate on it as Jubal suggested.'

Allard nodded, not all that interested, but saw she was frowning.

'I was surprised Jubal wrote in such detail about mounting that plate – it must've meant a good deal to him.'

Allard hadn't particularly noticed but didn't want to destroy her illusions. 'Yeah, I think he was proud of it.'

'Can you help me get it off, Jim? These rivets or screws don't seem to want to come out.'

He had to take his knife blade and prise under the edges, trying not to mark the newly dressed leather. It was difficult but the plate began to lift slowly and suddenly *pinged* as it jumped free. Allard tried to catch it, missed, and it clattered on the porch. He stooped to pick it up and when he straightened he saw Ella's face – pale, shocked.

'What's wrong?'

'Look!'

She put her hand into the hole left by removing the plate and pulled out a wad of folded greenbacks.

'The saddle's stuffed with money! There must be hundreds here!'

When they had it all out – the padding had been removed from the under-saddle and replaced with wads of bills – they counted almost thirteen thousand dollars.

Ella sat back, eyes wide, still in shock.

There was even a note from Jubal.

Sis, don't worry about where all this came from. I've been gathering it for years – for you. Anything here has already been paid back by insurance companies. Don't let that old conscience keep you awake nights!
Your Wayward Brother, Jubal

Of course she took quite a deal of convincing that it was all right for her to use the money and Allard knew she still worried over it.

Until, one morning, she came down to the corral where he was saddling the bay, ready for a ride down to Mexico with the seed bulls, bound for d'Angelo's ranch.

'Jim, I'll ride with you as far as town.' He looked quizzically at her, then nodded. 'I-I'm going to the bank. And pay back some of the money I borrowed.'

He smiled. 'At last! See, not so hard, is it?'

'I-I don't know, but I thought well, Jubal must have risked his life to get some of this, however he did get it, and he did it for me. I can't just ignore that. He demonstrated his love for me in the only way he knew how.'

Well, that was one way of looking at it . . .

'You're doing the right thing, Ella, just accept it, for whatever reason you like.'

She nodded, then looked at him. 'Saddle the black for me, will you, Jim? I-I think I might ride part of the way with you to Mexico. Perhaps all the way. . . .'

He grinned. 'Now that *is* the right thing to do – no question about it.'

Her laugh told him she agreed.